TRISH FOR PRESIDENT

TRISH FOR PRESIDENT

Lael Littke

Harcourt Brace Jovanovich, Publishers
San Diego   New York   London

Requests for permission to make copies of any part of the work should be
mailed to: Permissions, Harcourt Brace Jovanovich, Publishers,
Orlando, Florida 32887

Library of Congress Cataloging in Publication Data
Littke, Lael.
Trish for president.
Summary: Trish campaigns for junior class president in
an attempt to attract the romantic attentions of her
opponent and then finds that she has mixed feelings about
winning the election.
[1. Politics, Practical—Fiction. 2. Elections—Fiction.
3. Schools—Fiction] I. Title.
PZ7.L719Tr 1984   [Fic]   84-4587
ISBN 0-15-290512-X

Designed by G. B. D. Smith
Printed in the United States of America
First edition
A B C D E

For my mother, Ada, and my sister, Ivonne,
who have always been there

TRISH FOR PRESIDENT

1

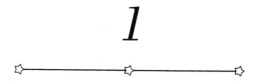

I GUESS I SHOULD BE GLAD that Snyde didn't sink a fang or two into Susu. I was mad enough to bite her myself. She had it coming. But even the way it was, Snyde almost wiped out my chances of getting anywhere in our class election.

I can't really blame Snyde for what happened. I mean, he only acted like what he is, which is a dog. He's a variety-store kind of dog, part boxer and part a whole lot of other breeds. He looks a lot like the picture of George Washington on a dollar bill. He's sweet and gentle, but he's also enormous, and I guess that's what got both of us into trouble.

On the other hand, what he did wouldn't have mattered a lot if I hadn't decided, the second semester of my sophomore year, to run for junior-class president. And I wouldn't have decided to run if I hadn't been in love with Jordan Avery. Everything's connected, like the foot bone's connected to the ankle bone, and the ankle bone's connected to the leg bone, and all that. One thing leads to another.

Maybe it was dumb of me to try for a school office in the first place. Even my best friend, Dannalee Davis, thought so. We were on the Wolf Creek school bus heading home on a Friday afternoon when I told her I had filed my intent to run.

"Trish Harker, are you off your spool?" Dannalee asked. "Who'll vote for you?"

Tact isn't Dannalee's best thing.

"Well," I fumbled, "you for one. I hope."

"Sure, me." Dannalee yanked up the sliding shoulder of her blouse. She's into bag-lady fashions, and you're never sure if her clothes are going to come along with her. "So you've got two votes. Mine and yours. And probably R. G. Cole's."

She twitched her head toward the back of the school bus where R. G. sat with his tuba and the rest of the guys. That's the way it is on our bus. The guys and girls don't mix much.

"It was R. G.'s idea that I ought to run," I said. "He passed around the petition for the fifty signatures. I don't think I would have done it on my own."

Dannalee nodded. "So, okay, you do have a few votes lined up. But you'll need a whole lot more. Do you realize who'll be running against you?"

The school bus was lumbering along the bank of the creek that gave our town its name. Wolf Creek comes rattling down from the mountains the same as we do each morning. It flows into Bear River just north of Pratt, which is where we, like the creek, flow into something bigger— namely Pratt High School. That's where I was going to be running for class president, and, yes, I did know who else was running. Jordan Avery, that's who. Jordan Avery, political genius of Pratt High.

Jordan will probably be running for president of the U. S. as soon as he's old enough. He's already let it be known that he's going to run for president of the Associated Student Body in our senior year, and he's out to win junior-class president so he can build his power base. Words like *power base* and *campaign strategy* and *opinion survey* fall from Jordan's tongue like ripe plums from a loaded tree.

Jordan, the brilliant.

Jordan, the popular.

Jordan, the love of my life.

The trouble was, Jordan didn't even know I was alive.

I sighed and looked away from Wolf Creek, back to Dannalee. "Jordan's running, and that's why nobody else would even try."

"Righto." Dannalee leaned a little closer, and I could smell the spearmint gum she was chewing. "Do you know who his campaign manager is?"

"I can guess." Anyone wanting to smear the competition all over the landscape would surely pick Susu Smith as campaign manager. You'd better not have any skeletons in the closet or even bad breath if you're going to tangle with Susu. That's why Arlene McKenna lost when she ran against Susu for soph-class secretary. Bad breath, I mean. Not because she has it, but because of what she does so she won't have it.

Arlene always carries this big plastic bottle of green mouthwash in her purse. Six or seven times a day she goes into the girls' rest room, takes a swig, and gurgles it around in the back of her throat. During the campaign, Susu and her committee put up this big green poster shaped like a mouth-wash bottle. On it was printed, "We urg-urg-urg you to vote for Susu Smith."

The principal made Susu take the poster down, but everybody had seen it already. Arlene hardly got any votes at all. People don't vote for the school joke.

"I imagine Jordan got Susu Smith to be his campaign manager," I said to Dannalee.

Dannalee looked at me sympathetically. "So why do you want to run?" she asked softly. "If you want to get flattened, walk in front of a truck. Why don't you just stick to giving speeches and writing articles for the school paper? You're good at that. Hey, why don't you run for editor? Why tackle trouble like Jordan and Susu?"

"I don't know." I looked out at the creek again and at the spring-green mountains in the background. "Maybe it's because I've never done anything significant before. If I win, I'll have something to put under my picture in the yearbook when we're seniors two years from now. If we were graduating this year, I could rent out the space under my picture. I haven't done anything worth mentioning."

Dannalee narrowed her eyes. "Come on, Trish. What's the real reason?"

The school bus was climbing now, up into the Idaho hills to the valley where Dannalee and I and the other riders live. I listened to the motor labor as I strained my brain to think of an answer for Dannalee. I couldn't tell her the truth. She didn't know how I felt about Jordan. To Dannalee, I'm sure it didn't seem at all sensible for me to run, and not just because Jordan and Susu were such operators. There were a lot of other things that would make it hard for me to win. Things like being from Wolf Creek, almost twenty miles from Pratt. It isn't easy for us Wolf Creek students to take part in extracurricular activities. Then there is the little problem of Pratt High being practically the world's capital of male chauvinism. Maybe that's because the main industries around Pratt are ranching and farming and lumbering. The guys have to be strong, and they like to run the world.

But here's the thing. Jordan goes for strong women. I mean, women with strong personalities. I'm running because I want him to think of me that way. I don't even have to win, as long as I conduct a bright, showy campaign so he'll know I'm around. And the better my campaign is, the better he'll look when he wins. Jordan will like that.

I couldn't tell all that to Dannalee. "I don't know," I said. "Maybe it's because no girl in our class has ever been president. Maybe it's because my sister was homecoming queen a few years ago and my brother was Preferred Man last year and I've always been just Gloria and Marv's dumpy little sister."

"Dumpy!" Dannalee said. "Trish, there are a lot of adjectives I could hang on you, but dumpy isn't one of them."

Well, okay, so dumpy isn't too accurate. But the other adjectives I would apply to myself aren't much better. Lanky. Freckled. Light-brown haired. (Gloria and Marv both have glossy black hair and alongside them I look faded.) Tall. I'm five feet nine inches, almost exactly the same as Jordan— which makes me *too* tall.

I sighed. "Cancel dumpy."

Dannalee grinned. "Don't sweat it, Trish. It doesn't matter *why* you're running, anyway. Just let me know how I can help. Who's going to manage your campaign?"

I glanced toward the back of the bus again. R. G. was

5

tooting his tuba in time to some music from Gordie Coons' transistor radio.

"R. G. is going to be my campaign manager," I said. "Since it was his idea in the first place, I figured he ought to have the job."

We were almost to Dannalee's stop. She stood up as she said, "He'll do a great job. I'm better at making posters and stuff like that." She started toward the door as the bus slowed. "What's the schedule for the campaign?"

I projected a calendar onto the wide screen of my brain. "Okay, today is Friday. Campaigning starts a week from Monday and goes through Thursday, when the election assembly is. We vote on that Friday, two weeks from today." I raised my voice as she got off. "We have only next week to get ready. We need to get together to make plans."

"Okay." As the bus started moving again, Dannalee ran alongside, talking through the open window. "I was wondering how come R. G. wants *you* to run."

I waved to her as we rolled away. The truth was that I didn't know why R. G. wanted me to run. He had found me at noon that day, which was the last day to file, and said he would pass around the required petition and get fifty signatures if I would agree to run. "If anybody can put a dent in Jordan's political machine, you can," he said.

"Me?" I looked around to see if he was talking to somebody else. "How could *I* do *that?*"

R. G. rattled the petition sheet he held in one hand, indicating he was in a hurry. "For one thing, you're not afraid to get up in front of people and give speeches."

That was true. I was involved in the Model United Nations and a debate team we were trying to get going and a few other things. Sometimes I thought I would like to be a lawyer someday and plead cases in front of juries and that kind of thing.

"Do you think there are fifty people who would sign that petition?" I asked.

"There are a lot of people who would like to put *somebody* up against Jordan." He rattled the paper again. "I don't have much time."

So I had agreed to do it, knowing R. G. didn't like Jordan and wondering if he was just using me as a weapon against him while he controlled me from the background.

I glanced back at R. G. now, expecting some sinister motive to be sticking out all over him. His cheeks were all puffed out from tooting his tuba, but his face was populated only by his freckles and a few Oreo cookie crumbs. Those guys back there were always eating.

Shame on me for suspecting R. G. He was my friend. We had lived on adjoining farms since we were babies.

But what were his motives? And could I make a decent showing just by being good at giving speeches? That's the thing that troubled me. I had no idea about how to run a campaign. What were R. G., Dannalee, and I going to do that would look good against Jordan and Susu and their friends?

It was like sending a few bows and arrows out against a dense pack of MX missiles.

The next day was Saturday, and that's when Snyde got into the act.

My brother Marv was home from college that weekend, and Dad asked him to drive our old truck to Pratt to get

7

a load of chicken feed. We keep about a thousand chickens on our farm, as well as a couple dozen cows and a few horses. We raise alfalfa and grain to feed the animals, but the chickens need some other things like calcium and some stuff called "mash." Dad's really into chicken nutrition.

"Want to go along to Pratt for the ride, Trish?" Marv asked while we were eating breakfast, which was stacks of Mom's famous flapjacks smothered in her famous home-made gooseberry jam. I skated a hunk of flapjack around my plate to coat it with jam while I thought about Marv's question.

I knew he needed me to go along with him to stack the heavy sacks of chicken feed as he hoisted them into the truck. He knew I knew the real reason he was asking me, and I knew he knew I knew. Marv is always telling me I should be more feminine, which means I should wear ruffles and giggle and look helpless. That's the kind of girl Marv likes. But you can bet he never turns down a hand with the heavy work. He never comes right out and asks me to help him clean the barn or drive the tractor. He knows I'll do it if he asks me to come along "for the ride," because I know what he's really asking.

"Sure, Marv," I said. "I'll go along with you. Just for the ride."

To tell the truth, I'd rather sling sacks of chicken feed around than scrub floors and plant radishes, which is what Mom would have me doing if I stayed home.

We started out in the battered old farm truck with Snyde sitting between us. Snyde has a little trouble with his self-image. He thinks being treated like a dog is a put-down, so when he rides in the truck he sits right up on the seat looking out the windshield like anybody else. Once Marv put a wig on him and told people he was our Aunt Beulah. He took him to school that way. The kids really liked Snyde, and for a long time they asked how our Aunt Beulah was.

Marv talked about applied hen psychology as we sped along the highway. He's trying to decide whether to major in animal husbandry or psychology. Sometimes I think he gets the two things mixed up.

"It doesn't take much to keep a hen happy," Marv was saying. "Just give her some clean straw to scratch in and keep the food coming regularly. She'll love you for it and do her thing, which is an egg a day."

I think Marv sees things too simply. It's my job to gather the eggs each day, clean them, and put them into the egg crates that are picked up by the egg-company truck every Tuesday. I know there are a lot of hens who don't perform every day. And there are a lot of others who peck at your hands when you try to take the eggs.

"Well," I said, "hens aren't exactly my favorite subject for study."

Marv laughed. "What you should be studying, Trish, is home economics, so you can make some man a good wife someday."

Marv is always telling me I should study home economics like our sister Gloria did. He says that's the only sensible thing for a girl to study.

"I think I'm going to study law." I like to mention that to Marv whenever the subject comes up, just to bug him. I'm not absolutely sure what I'm going to do. I'd even study home ec if it would make Jordan happy. But his mother is a lawyer, and I've heard him say several times how much he admires her.

"Law!" Marv snorted. "You can't put law on the table when your hungry man comes home."

I shrugged. "So maybe *he'll* study home economics."

We bickered all the way to the feed store in Pratt.

I really worked up a sweat loading the calcium and mash with Marv. That didn't do much for my appearance, which wasn't going to set any fashion fads in the first place. My baggy blue T-shirt advertised Lub-Mor Axle Grease and my jeans were on the downhill side of faded. That's why I stayed in the truck when Marv parked in front of O. P. Skaggs to get groceries for Mom. I had never worried much about my public image before, but now that I was running for office, I didn't want to be seen looking like that. Especially I didn't want to be seen by Jordan, who just might be shopping for something.

They have slant parking in Pratt, so Snyde and I had a moving-picture view of the street. Snyde thumped his tail when we saw R. G. go past. I figured he had brought his old car to McCabe's Auto Repair Shop again. He calls the car "Belch" because that's about all it does when he tries to start it. It's pretty much a live-in at McCabe's. R. G. worked on it for a year before he turned sixteen last month, but I think the only place he has driven it is to the shop.

A couple other kids from school went past, and then I saw Susu Smith come out of Johnson's Drugstore and head down the street toward us. I quickly ducked my head behind Snyde's big shoulders, but Susu had already seen me. She came over to the driver's side of the truck, probably hoping Marv was in there somewhere. All the girls like Marvelous Marv.

"Hi, Trish." Susu's eyes slid over the dents and manure that decorated the truck. "In the big city for the day?"

"No," I said. "Just here in little old Pratt."

Susu hates to be reminded that Pratt isn't one of the world's top pleasure spots. It's a great place, really, and I would never knock it. But Susu is always calling Dannalee and me "hicks from the sticks" and things like that. I knew I shouldn't have smarted off to her that way, but my mouth is faster than my brain.

Susu continued to smile. "I don't think I've met your boyfriend." She looked straight at Snyde. "But I must say, you make a *very* good couple." She reached into the truck to tweak Snyde's ear.

Snyde was watching a German shepherd dog who was watering a lamppost in back of Susu. Just as she touched him, Snyde lifted his upper lip and showed his fangs. I'm sure he was doing it for the benefit of the German shepherd, but Susu squealed and jumped back. That rattled the German shepherd, who began to bark right behind her. Snyde translated the bark as a threat. Just as Susu leaped forward to get away from the shepherd, Snyde opened his big mouth and poured his bass voice and a lot of spit all over her.

Susu started yelping louder than the dogs. "Help! Help!" she squealed. "Get him away from me!"

People began running toward us. The shepherd was boiling around the lamppost, stopping every now and then to water it a little more. All the while, he kept barking up a storm, begging for a fight. Snyde leaned out of the driver's window, letting him know he was willing. I had my arms around Snyde's middle, but he had his front paws outside the window and was baying in Susu's face.

Susu was getting hysterical. "You did it!" she yelled,

pointing at me. "You set him on me. And I was just trying to be friendly!"

Some friendly. Susu has the personality of a scrub brush. Friendly to her is taking someone's skin off.

Around Snyde's haunches I saw R. G. pushing his way to the front of the crowd. Somebody collared the shepherd and towed him off down the street. R. G. took hold of Susu's arm, trying to haul her back from Snyde's dripping jaws.

Susu yanked her arm away. "Get your mitts off me," she hollered. "It's bad enough to be attacked by a *dog!*"

"Snyde wasn't attacking you." R. G. reached out to push the dog back inside the truck cab with me. "Didn't you see the German shepherd? Snyde wouldn't hurt anybody."

"Oh, yeah?" Susu's volume went up a couple of decibels. "What do you know about it, you big blister?"

Snyde, seeing his enemy disappearing down the street, delivered a final volley of barks. Susu let out another squeal.

A man on my side of the truck said, "Ought to be locked up, a vicious beast like that."

Another guy snickered. "Which one, the dog or the girl?"

That really made Susu sputter. She moved up almost nose to nose with Snyde, giving him back snarl for bark. I was sharing the window with Snyde, trying to keep him wedged inside the truck.

As I struggled with Snyde, I saw Riley McQuaid jumping around the crowd, trying to aim that big camera he always carries with him. Riley takes pictures for our school newspaper and sometimes for the *Pratt Bugle*, which we call the *Pratt Blatt*. If he got a picture of me now, it might turn up anywhere.

I didn't have time to worry about that, though, because just then I heard the whine of a police-car siren. That would be Earl Traxler. He's Pratt's chief of police, although since it's a one-man police force, he has nobody to chief over.

Susu, who was building up steam for her next bellow at Snyde and me, let out her breath with a gust. She smiled. "Just you wait, Trish Harker. Just you wait."

Above the siren I thought I heard a faint *glug-glug-glug*. It wasn't Arlene McKenna and her mouthwash. It was my hopes for conducting a classy campaign slowly disappearing down the drain. Susu isn't one to forgive and forget.

2

I WANT TO SAY RIGHT OFF that Traxler is okay. Off duty, he's really kind of nice. But there's something about stuffing himself into that tight-fitting uniform with the gunbelt slung around his hips that makes him feel important. He doesn't have a whole lot to do since Pratt isn't exactly crawling with criminals, so he's always on the lookout for something to relieve his boredom. He comes down hard on teenagers, probably because he remembers what *he* was like in his teens.

"Awright, awright," he bellowed, burning rubber as he skidded the black-and-white car to a stop. "What's going on here? How come I can't even go in for a bite of lunch without all hell breaking loose?"

He heaved himself out of the car. Using his potbelly as a battering ram, he waded into the crowd.

Nobody except Snyde said anything. Why is it that dogs hate uniforms? Snyde went into a frenzy. Turning his volume to full output, he lunged forward, succeeding in getting almost three-fourths of himself out of the window. I nearly smashed some ribs on the steering wheel, trying to hold on to what was left of him inside the truck.

Traxler put his hand on the butt of his gun. "Whose dog is that?" he demanded.

"Hers." Susu, her cute little round chin quivering, extended a finger toward me. All her bristle was gone.

Traxler gently pushed her behind him as Snyde aimed a new batch of snarls at him. Jockeying around so that he could see me behind Snyde's hindquarters, he yelled, "Get that beast out of here or I'll shoot him."

"Aw, hell, Earl," a man in the crowd said, "the mutt was just having a little barking contest with Old Whipper. No harm done."

"Old Whipper? I don't see him anywheres around." Traxler peered belligerently up the street, but at least he took his hand off his gun.

"Somebody hauled him off," the man said. "You know how he's always wandering the streets."

Susu stuck her head out from behind Traxler. "That *dog* attacked me, Mr. Traxler," she whimpered. Her stabbing finger pointed more at me than at Snyde.

I don't know what would have happened next if Marv hadn't come out of O. P. Skaggs just then, his arms loaded with two bags of groceries.

"Hey, what happened?" he said, running toward the truck. "Is Trish all right? What's the matter with Snyde?"

I have to give him credit for thinking of me first.

Snyde shut up when he saw Marv. He started his tail going, whapping me rhythmically in the face. Whining, he stretched toward Marv.

"Didn't you hear the war going on out here?" I yowled. "Where have you been?"

"I was back in the meat locker." Marv pushed his way to the truck and dumped the bags of groceries in the back. "Now will somebody give me a clue as to what happened?"

Susu, R. G., and I all spoke at once. Snyde got in a little heavy breathing and a couple of face licks when Marv moved close to him. Marv turned his head from one person to the other, as if he were watching a three-sided tennis match. Gradually his attention focused on Susu, and he gazed at her as if she were one of Mom's famous fresh-peach pies smothered in whipped cream.

I squinted at Susu, trying to see if she had changed that much in the year since Marv graduated from Pratt High. He had never noticed her while he was there, but of course, seniors don't see freshmen.

"Marv," Susu quavered, "I was so-o-o-o scared." Leaving Traxler's protection, she wound herself around Marv.

Traxler stood there taking in the whole scene. I could almost see the thought processes going on in his head. Marv had never given him a whole lot of trouble. Snyde was a first offender. Susu was cute, and she was happy now that she had Marv to perform for. The crowd had had a good show, and he himself had had an opportunity to demonstrate his authority.

"This your rig, Marv?" he asked. His eyes flicked over me, Snyde, and the cruddy truck, including us all in the same category.

Marv nodded, his eyes pasted on Susu.

"Well, get it out of here or I'll have to impound that mutt."

Marv's gaze shifted to Traxler. "I'll do that, sir. I'm sorry he caused such a fuss."

"Well," Traxler growled, "just leave him home next time."

"Right. Thanks, Officer Traxler." Marv turned back to Susu. "I'm awfully sorry about this. I hope Snyde didn't hurt you."

I hugged Snyde. I wanted to say that if anybody was hurt, it was the rest of us, who were suffering ear damage from all of Susu's squealing. But I kept my mouth shut.

Susu played it for all it was worth. Holding out her soft, round arms, she anxiously looked at them. Then she raised her skirt, just a smidge, and peeked at her cute little legs. "I think I'm okay, Marv. Maybe you'd better look me over."

Marv looked her over. His Adam's apple trembled. A low whistle came from some other guy in the crowd.

"I'd better drive you home, Susu," Marv said.

Susu dropped her skirt and bounced a glance off me and Snyde and the manure-spattered truck. "I'll be fine, Marv, but maybe you could come back down later and see how I'm doing."

"Hell, buddy," some guy said, "if you don't, I will."

"I'll call you, Susu," Marv said.

Traxler started whuffing at the crowd. "Show's over," he said. "Everybody go home."

Susu glided off with the others. "See you later, Marv," she said. Then she looked at me. "Bye, Trish. See you Monday."

The way she said it didn't exactly make me look forward to Monday.

Marv got into the truck and started it. R. G. hammered

on the door at my side. "How about a hitch home?" he asked. "My car has to stay at McCabe's for a few days."

"So what else is new?" Marv motioned for him to get in, so I opened the door.

R. G. climbed in as I shoved Snyde over to make room. "McCabe's going to tell me if it's worth fixing any more. I've already replaced almost everything in it." He slammed the door and settled in.

"Wouldn't it be cheaper just to get another car?" Marv asked as he backed out of the parking space and headed toward Wolf Creek.

R. G. nodded. "I guess so. But I like it."

R. G.'s car was a 1957 Chevy convertible with tail fins. It was the ugliest thing on the road, but he kept it shined and polished, even though it hardly ever ran.

Marv stopped at the only red light in Pratt, just in time for Susu to cross the street in front of us. He gave her a little toot on the horn, and she smiled and waved. "See you later," she mouthed.

Even Snyde watched as she flowed her way to the opposite curb.

"That girl has a tongue that could sand lumber," R. G. said.

Marv looked surprised. "Susu? She was real nice to *me*."

"Sure," I said. "All the girls are nice to Marvelous Marvy."

That was mean, and I knew it. But I was really ticked at Marv for falling for Susu's routine.

"Hey," Marv said as the light turned green and he started up again, "you don't think I fell for her act, do you? Give me a break, Trish. I've been around the block a couple of times."

So maybe he wasn't as dumb as I thought he was. "I'm sorry, Marv. I really thought you were going for her."

Marv sent me a quick grin past Snyde's muzzle. "Trouble with you, Trish, is that you don't know how to play the game."

Trouble with me was that I didn't even know there *was* a game.

"If there were more girls like Trish," R. G. said, "people wouldn't *have* to play games."

"Thanks, R. G." It was nice to have a cheering section, even if it was only R. G. I shifted to make more room for him, hoping my deodorant hadn't failed.

We were out of Pratt by then, and Marv poured on a little speed as he headed up Indian Ridge. "Trish," he said, his eyes on the winding road, "how about letting me in on what's going on between you and Susu? You both after the same guy or something?"

I twisted around so I could see past Snyde. "Contrary to your Big College Jock opinion, Marv, some girls think of other things than how to snag a guy." I felt like kind of a hypocrite saying that because my whole aim in life was to catch Jordan's attention. But Marv was making me mad again. Besides, when Susu got through with me, after today's little episode, my chances of getting Jordan to like me were nowhere.

"Wouldn't hurt you, Trish, to think a little more about such things. The female of the species sometimes wears a dress and lets a guy open a door for her."

"Great," I said. "Next time the barn needs mucking out, I'll put on a dress and let you open the door before I start shoveling out the stuff."

Marv took a hand off the steering wheel to push back

my flow of words. "Okay, okay, okay. I get the point. Now will you tell me what's with you and Susu? I might even be able to help, you know."

"Doesn't he know about the election?" R. G. said into my right ear.

I shook my head and then said to Marv, "The thing is, I'm running for junior-class president."

"Against Susu?" Marv's tone left no doubt as to who he thought would win.

"No. Against Jordan Avery. Susu is his campaign manager."

"So that's it." Marv thought about it a minute. "Why don't you just withdraw and let some guy run against Jordan? He's pretty heavy competition. You could run for secretary."

I was getting steamed. I didn't know whether it was because I was jammed so close to Snyde and R. G. or because Marv's attitude was rebuilding familiar fires inside me.

I gritted my teeth. "I'm running for *president.* If Susu does a hatchet job on me, I'll just have to fall down and bleed awhile before I get on with it. But I'm going to try." I was going to show Marv that a girl *could* make a good showing against a guy like Jordan. To heck with Susu. I'd think of some way to take care of her.

"Okay," Marv said. "Maybe I can smooth things over with Susu. About today, I mean." Suddenly he whistled between his teeth. "Susu's the one who did the mouthwash job on Arlene McKenna last year, isn't she?"

"The same." I pushed Snyde off my lap. He had spotted a cat outside and was leaning across me, breathing in my face, dripping spit all over my jeans. "Speaking of mouthwash," I said, "Snyde could use some."

"What he needs is a dose of Tidy Bowl." R. G. leaned out the window for a breath of unpolluted air. "Wouldn't hurt to let Marv see what he can do, Trish." His words were almost blown away in the breeze.

Maybe it was the whiff of dog breath that made me imagine the stink Susu was probably going to raise about Snyde and me. Suddenly I felt tired. Maybe I *couldn't* hack it. "Maybe I *should* just forget the whole thing," I said.

"Hey, Trish, don't go into a tailspin." Marv's tone was upbeat now. "You've always been like a phoenix, you know. You crash in flames one day, but the next day you're up and at it again. Don't let this thing with Susu wipe you out."

"He talks like a college guy," R. G. whispered in my ear.

"Yeah," I agreed. "What's a phoenix, R. G.?"

R. G. shrugged. "I dunno. I think it's a place in Arizona."

Mrs. Toomey from across the road waved to me while Marv and I unloaded the chicken feed at home. If I have a fan club, I guess it's Mrs. Toomey. She thinks I'm "such a nice young girl" and that I'm "just wonderful" for working so hard around the farm.

Mrs. Toomey works hard, too. She must be close to eighty, and has lived alone since her children grew up and left and her husband died.

I waved back to her, thinking I should go visit with her and tell her all about the coming election. She's interested in things like that.

She was on her way out to gather eggs from the few hens she keeps, and as she walked she sang, "Now let us rejoice in the day of salvation, no longer as strangers on earth need we roam. . . ." You can always gauge how Mrs. Toomey is feeling by her choice of hymns for the day. This was a happy one. I told myself I would go visit her as soon as I could.

When Marv and I had finished unloading, I went into the house and looked up "phoenix." The dictionary said it was a mythical bird that rises from its own ashes and lives through another cycle of years. I still didn't know what Marv meant by calling me a phoenix, but I guess I was flattered. He can be nice sometimes. I have to say this for Marv. He has something to show for his four years in high school. The list of his accomplishments under his senior picture practically runs off the page.

But he never ran for class office.

It would be really terrific if I could put "Junior-Class President" under my senior picture. As long as I was having fantasies, why not make it big? Why not add "Associated Student Body President," too? I projected it on the wide screen of my mind. Why not? Today, Pratt high. Tomorrow, the world!

Jordan would be dazzled! Or would he?

Marv called Susu after he finished his outside work. I heard him tell her he'd be by about seven-thirty.

"It's just to help you out, Trish," he said when he got off the phone. "I'll let her talk things out. Then she'll forget about what happened today and won't use it against you."

"Sure, Marv." I wondered if he was as savvy about girls as he thought he was. I considered offering to go along to protect *him* from Susu, but there are some things a person has to learn for himself.

I spent the afternoon helping Mom with the housework. Mom has this big thing about getting the house ready for

Sunday. Every Saturday we scrub the kitchen floor and vacuum all the carpets. We dust and polish the furniture. We wash the windows. Mom gets a large charge from looking at a clean and sparkling house. It *is* kind of nice, like starting a new week fresh, without being loaded down by last week's problems.

While we worked, I told Mom about what had happened in Pratt that day and what effect it might have on the election.

"There's a Susu in every class," Mom said. "In my class her name was Franny. She would smear anybody to get what she wanted."

I flipped my dust cloth expertly over the seat of a chair. "Did you ever tangle with Franny, Mom?"

Mom laughed. "No, I wasn't into school politics. I thought girls like Franny were pushy."

Pushy? Would Jordan like pushy?

"Mom," I asked, "am I pushy?"

"You're nothing like Franny, Trish. Or Susu." Mom sprayed a tabletop with polish, then paused. "Looking back, I'm not sure Franny was all that pushy. She wanted to be student body president, and in those days it was pretty hard for a girl. Maybe she wouldn't have been so mean if some of the rest of us had supported her. But we were afraid the guys wouldn't like it."

"I don't know that things have changed that much," I said glumly. "At least at Pratt High."

Mom leaned over and attacked the tabletop with her cloth. "Maybe not. But I'm glad you're making a stab at it, and I hope you run a good, straight campaign. I'm really proud of you, Trish. Sometimes. . . ." She paused again. "Sometimes I wish I had done more with my own life."

That surprised me. Mom has always seemed so happy with what she does. She really takes momming seriously. She has always tried to teach Gloria and me the things that will make us good homemakers. Gloria went for it. Right out of high school, she married R. G.'s older brother, Blaine. Now they have this cute baby they call "Junior."

But I'm not sure I want to do the same thing. Unless, of course, I'm going to marry Jordan.

Even then I'm not sure. I had a really bad thought, one that made me feel as if I had just touched a decayed place in my brain. It was that I didn't want to be like my mom. I mean, she's the greatest and I love the way she makes our whole family so comfortable and takes care of the house and all. I want the same kind of home for the family I will have someday.

But I don't want to say, when I'm Mom's age, that I wish I had done more with my life.

It reminds me of that TV commercial where the mother stands beside herself and wonders if her daughter cares about the wash. Then the daughter comes and admires how nice her cheerleading outfit is, and the mother gets all hyper and says, "She *does* care about the wash."

Well, I do care about the wash. But I'm not sure I want to be the one who *does* it all the time, if you know what I mean.

Maybe running for class office would be the thing that would show me which way I wanted to go.

3

MARV LEFT FOR HIS DATE with Susu just before seven p.m.
I snickered a little to myself when he borrowed Dad's Buick
to drive. No smelly farm truck or even Marv's little red
Veedub Bug for Susu. He couldn't tell me he wasn't out to
impress her.

Before he left, he assured me again that he would wipe
that day's episode completely from Susu's mind.

"No sweat, Trish," he said. "Let big brother Marv take
care of it."

Okay, so maybe he could. Marv is your basic, everyday,
run-of-the-mill Prince Charming. He's tall and thin, and his
gorgeous dark hair falls in his eyes a lot. People like him,
especially girl people.

So if he was going to take care of that, I needed to get
moving on other aspects of my campaign.

I called Dannalee.

I knew she'd be home. Dannalee and I don't date much.
The Wolf Creek guys don't go out much with the Wolf

Creek girls. After seeing us mucking out a barn or breaking our backs over a potato patch, they prefer the Pratt girls who play tennis and sit around Hanna's Sweet Shoppe. R. G. did take me to a school dance last year. When he took me home, he got carried away and kissed me. After that he didn't look at me on the school bus for a week, and he hasn't asked me for another date. That says a lot for my kissing. I guess I'll never be Miss Passion Pit of Pratt High.

The Pratt guys don't date Wolf Creek girls except the super-cute ones. I guess they figure it's too much trouble to drive twenty miles to pick up a girl, drive twenty miles back to Pratt for a movie or school dance, and then reverse the whole thing at the end of the date.

"Hi," I said when Dannalee answered the phone. "Doing anything tonight?"

"Well." Dannalee's voice was low and breathy over the phone. "A dark stranger is picking me up in an hour, and we're flying to Paris for a love-filled weekend. So what are *you* doing?"

"Wishing," I said. "Same as you. So maybe you and I and R. G. could get together and start thinking up fantastic things for my campaign."

Dannalee groaned. "Wish I could. But Mom's come down with a new romance."

I knew what she meant. Her mom is always coming down with romances. It isn't that she runs around with men. She *writes* romances. As far as I know, she has never sold any. But when she's in the midst of writing one, dinner time, Sunday, and the Fourth of July can pass by without her noticing. During those times, it's up to Dannalee to excavate through all the dirty dishes and find the kitchen stove so that the family gets fed. She does that besides helping her dad with the chores. Dannalee is the youngest of three girls in the family and the only one left at home.

"How about tomorrow?" I asked. I could already feel time slipping away from us, with no plans for a spectacular campaign.

Dannalee groaned again. "We're all going to Pocatello to celebrate my grandma's birthday. Sorry, Trish. Can we get together Monday after school?"

"Sure, okay, Dannalee. Don't worry about it."

"Maybe R. G. could come over and the two of you could get some ideas," Dannalee offered.

"Maybe I'll give him a call." But I knew I wouldn't.

I didn't. My relationship with R. G. has changed since that night he kissed me. Since then I haven't called him and asked him to come over to play Scrabble or Uno or something. He still comes over now and then, but I don't *ask* him anymore.

I spent the evening with a pencil and a sheet of paper headed: "Things I Can Do So Jordan Will Think I Am Sophisticated and Interesting."

When I went to bed, the paper was still blank.

Marv got up early the next morning to help Dad with the chores, then went back to bed. He was too zonked to go to church with the rest of us, so I had to wait until later to find out what had happened with Susu.

At church, R. G. slid into the empty seat beside me and immediately began scribbling notes.

"Is Marv driving back to the university this afternoon?" the first note read.

"Yes," I scribbled back.

R. G. applied pencil to paper again. "Would he let me

ride into Pratt with him? McCabe called and said he's done all he can for Belch short of a complete engine transplant. Wants me to get it out of his shop because he has others coming in."

"Ask Marv," I penciled back. I really wasn't in the mood for pass-the-note. I hadn't slept well the night before. I kept seeing Susu's poison looks at me and thinking I didn't have any antidote.

"Why don't you come to Pratt with me?" R. G.'s next note said. "On the way back, we can talk about the campaign."

"Sounds good," I wrote back.

It made me feel a little better to think we'd be getting something going. But I still couldn't concentrate on the day's sermon. Instead I flipped through the hymnbook and ran across one of those "treasure hunts" that kids write in hymnals when they're bored in church. At the bottom of a page was written, "What did Kenny say when he proposed to Lisa? See page 51."

I turned to page fifty-one. The name of that hymn was "Abide With Me." Ha, ha.

At the bottom of that page was written, "What was Bill's condition after he hiked up Mt. Baldy and smoked pot? Turn to page 62."

Dutifully I turned to page sixty-two. The hymn was "High on the Mountain Top." Not bad. I looked at the question at the bottom of that page. "What is Tom Harding's theme song? Turn to page 260."

I knew what to expect. Tom Harding is the keeper of Wolf Creek's general store. Sure enough, the hymn was "We Thank Thee O God for a Prophet," and *prophet* was changed to *profit*. That was an old one. Sighing, I closed the hymnbook and tried to concentrate on the sermon. The treasure hunt idea kept nipping at my mind. Maybe I could use it for my campaign. I filed it away.

Marv was whistling around the kitchen when I got home.

"That Susu's one neat chick," he said when I walked in. "Funny I never noticed her before."

"I guess you're at the age where you like younger *women*," I said. I emphasized "women" because I hate it when he refers to his girl friends as "chicks." But since I was hoping he had done me a favor, I didn't make a big thing of it this time.

I waited for him to say something about his talk with Susu, but he walked around peeking in the oven at the roast Mom had put in before we went to church and at the pot of boiling potatoes she had just fixed. "There's no cooking like home cooking," he warbled. "Man, I get sick of scraping together my own meals. Maybe I'll get married so I'll have someone to cook real food for me." He grinned amiably at me.

"Marv!" I said. "What did Susu say?"

His grin widened. "She said, 'Oh, Marvy, you're *just marv*elous!'" He made his voice high-pitched, like Susu's.

"Oh, come off it." Marv could be such a pain. "I mean about what happened yesterday. Did you talk her out of clubbing me with it?"

"Piece of cake," Marv said. "She's not the kind to carry a grudge. I explained how Snyde is a little much for you to handle, and she said she could see that. That's all there was to it."

Somehow I didn't think my problem was solved. But I said, "Thank you, Marv," and let it drop.

Marv got ready to drive back to the university right after we finished eating. I was helping him load his red Veedub with loaves of Mom's homemade bread, leftover roast beef, and half that day's rhubarb pie when I saw R. G. running across the fields that separate his dad's farm from ours. He played imaginary basketball as he ran, dribbling a phantom ball through the sprouting alfalfa and stopping now and then to sink an invisible basket. At least for once he had left his tuba at home. R. G. plays tuba in our school marching band, and he takes it with him whenever he can so he can practice at odd moments.

Marv was happy to have company as far as Pratt. Shoving the front seat forward, he motioned for me to get in back. I thought R. G. would sit up front with Marv, and I think Marv did, too. But he crawled in back with me, even though he had to put a couple folds in his legs to fit.

That left the passenger seat in front empty, and Snyde invited himself to go along, showing his pleasure with a couple of joyful barks as he settled in.

I kicked the back of his seat. "Hey, get out, Snyde. You can't go."

"Aw, let the poor mutt come," Marv said. "He never has any fun."

"Seems to me he had too much fun yesterday," I complained. "Remember what Traxler said?"

"Traxler will be home taking his Sunday siesta." Marv leaned across Snyde and pulled the door shut, closed his own door, and started the car. "You'll be out of town before he even wakes up."

Mom came running out with a dozen eggs for Marv and instructions for him to drive carefully. Dad gave us a wave from the front porch, and then went inside for his own Sunday nap.

Marv let R. G., Snyde, and me off at McCabe's garage and took off. I noticed that he didn't head down the highway that led to the university. Instead, he turned in the direction of Susu's house.

Mr. McCabe was already there at the garage waiting for us. "It was all I could do to get 'er goin' again," he said, flipping a thumb at Belch. The clumsy car sat forlornly in the middle of a puddle of oil. "I done all I could, but she'll probably be back in here before I can blink an eye. She's had about all she can take with that engine."

"Guess I ought to trade it in on a horse," R. G. said. He patted Belch's shiny fender affectionately.

McCabe faked an alarmed look. "Gawd, son, don't do that. How'n hell am I gonna earn a living if you take away my main source of income?" He handed R. G. the key. "Get it out of here before it falls apart on my floor. I'll put it on your daddy's bill, as usual."

"I'll be selling a pig pretty soon," R. G. said. "I'll get it paid up."

"Know you will, son," Mr. McCabe said. "By then you'll have a couple more bills." He grinned at R. G. and me. "Cars and women. They'll keep you poor."

R. G. thanked Mr. McCabe and opened Belch's door for me and Snyde to get in. Snyde wanted to sit by the window, but I didn't want to cozy up to R. G., so I shoved him over.

Belch started up with a series of backfires that sounded like the bombardment of Fort McHenry. R. G. fed it a little gas and it lurched out onto the street. We started for home in jackrabbit leaps.

We hadn't gone more than a block when Traxler's black-and-white pulled up alongside us. "Shoulda known it was that tank of yours, Cole," he said to R. G. "Heard it clear down at the Burger Barn." He started to drive away.

I was trying to drape myself over Snyde somehow so that he wouldn't see Traxler. I had his eyes covered, but I guess he must have recognized the chief's voice. Or maybe he smelled the onions from Traxler's burger. Struggling out of my arms, Snyde poked his big snout out the window, aimed a snarl at Traxler, and fired it like a cannonball.

Traxler braked and pulled over close to us. "Hey," he bellowed. "Thought I told you snots to keep that mangy mutt off the streets."

I yanked Snyde back away from the window. "He's not on the streets. He's in the car."

Traxler moved his car closer to Belch. "Oh, now you're going to smart-ass it, eh? Well, how'd you like a ticket for contempt of the law?"

I was fried. We weren't doing anything except trying to get Belch out of Traxler's life. I opened my mouth to tell him so, but R. G. told me to cool it.

"Don't bug him," he said. "If I have to stop now, I'll never get Belch started again." He turned his face toward Traxler, and I think he smiled. "My car isn't dependable, Mr. Traxler. We brought Snyde along for protection in case we broke down somewhere in the boonies."

Traxler harrumphed. "Well, I don't want to see him around here again. Now, get that heap off the main drag."

"I'm trying," R. G. said between his teeth. He stepped on the gas. Belch lurched a couple of times and began to shake, as if it were going to collapse. But at least it kept going.

R. G. turned right. "Let's get off the 'main drag.' The way Traxler talks, we're creating a traffic jam when we're the only car on the street besides his."

The street we were on led past the city park. There was a bunch of high school kids lounging on the grass, and right in the middle of them was Jordan Avery.

Seeing him there was like spying a fantastic rainbow after a miserable storm.

Even from where I was, I could see the beautiful mole on his cheek and those laser eyes of his, those shining beams that can slice right through you. I think it is Jordan's eyes that give him his power. He's not movie-star handsome. He has thick brown hair and kind of shaggy eyebrows. Sometimes he has zits, just like everybody else. His lips are great, sort of like they were sculptured out of marble. But it's his eyes that really do things to you.

Oh, Jordan. I sent a silent message in his direction. *I can be the kind of girl you like, Jordan. Whatever kind of girl you like.*

As if in answer to my message, Jordan turned those laser eyes right on me. And just then Belch died with a lot of snorts and an embarrassing cloud of fumes. Jordan and a few of the other guys came over to see what was happening. Jordan came right over to my window as R. G. got out to raise the hood.

"Hi, Trish," he said.

He knew my name!

His eyes scorched me. "I heard that we're going for the same office." He smiled, increasing the intensity of those eyes.

My tongue was like a swollen gland filling my mouth. I tried to laugh, but it came out a whinny.

R. G. leaped back into the car and turned the key. Belch backfired and started. "Slam the hood," he yelled. "We're rolling."

I'm sure Jordan didn't think he had much competition. I hadn't gotten out a single word. I buried my face in Snyde's shoulder and tried to forget the whole scene.

We were rolling, all right—forty-seven miles per hour in a thirty-five mile per hour zone. Snyde crawled across me to stick his head out the window and let his tongue and his ears flap in the wind.

"Maybe we're rolling a little too much," I said.

"We're almost back to the highway." R. G. had been taking side streets so we wouldn't clutter up Traxler's 'main drag' but now we had to get back on the highway to get to Wolf Creek. "I don't dare slow up or we won't have enough momentum to get up Indian Ridge."

Barely slowing for a stop sign, R. G. swung onto the highway. Pouring on more gas, he laughed excitedly. "Old McCabe's all right. Belch hasn't had this much life since it rolled out of the factory."

Belch answered with a volley of backfires, but it kept rolling. We got to fifty-two miles per hour, then fifty-seven. Then sixty-five.

"Whee," R. G. chortled.

"Yeah, whee," I said. I had shot a look behind us, and it had scored a direct hit on Traxler's black-and-white. "Guess who's chasing us."

"Can't stop," R. G. said. "His jurisdiction ends in about a mile, anyway." He tromped a little harder on the gas pedal. "Maybe he's just escorting us out of town."

I didn't have to answer that because Traxler turned on his siren about then. And Belch began to lose speed.

"Come on, baby." R. G.'s face was flushed as he coaxed Belch to keep going.

The police car pulled closer. Snyde leaned out and shotgunned it with barks.

"We're not going to make it," I groaned.

"Yes, we are." R. G. was floorboarding it. But the slopes of Indian Ridge were too much for Belch. Backfiring and jackrabbiting, it was slowing to a stop.

"We're out of his jurisdiction," R. G. said as Belch coughed and died. We coasted to a stop. Dust swirled around us.

Traxler pulled alongside us, siren howling. Snyde barked.

"You going to mention it?" I asked R. G.

He shook his head.

Traxler turned off the siren, which must have impressed Snyde because he turned off his barks, too.

In the dusty silence, Traxler glared at us. "Smart-ass kids," he said. "Snots."

He opened the back door of the police car. "Get in," he said. "All three of you."

The courthouse is on the same street as the park. This time when we passed, Jordan and the other people were standing up, getting ready to leave. Susu was there. And Riley Mc-Quaid. And Riley's camera.

Susu pointed at us. Riley raised his camera. Jordan smiled and waved. I wondered if he liked tongue-tied girls who rode around in police cars.

So far my campaign was going all in the wrong direction.

35

4

THE THING I WAS MOST WORRIED ABOUT was that Riley Mc-Quaid had taken a picture. How would it look to have a candidate for class president shown peering from the backseat of Traxler's cop car? Susu could really do things with that.

However, this was one case where one thing didn't necessarily follow after another. Just because Riley got the picture didn't mean that it would automatically end up in Susu's hands. The fact that he was hanging around with Susu and Jordan didn't mean that he felt any particular loyalty to them. Riley is unpredictable. It's generally agreed around Pratt High that he's only about a week out of a tree. Riley would sell the negative to the person who dangled the most bananas in front of his face, if you know what I mean.

I guess R. G. was thinking the same thing. "I'd better call Riley as soon as I get home," he said.

That was a good thought, but there was a problem. "What'll you use for money? You've sunk all you have into

Belch. And my total wealth amounts to about eight dollars and fifty-nine cents. Riley knows a picture like that can bring at least fifteen dollars."

"Yeah." R. G. twisted around to look out the back window of the police car. "Besides, if I know Susu, she's probably already mortgaged her favorite set of daggers for that picture."

I sighed. "Maybe he couldn't focus fast enough. Maybe he didn't even get a picture."

Traxler half-turned his head back toward us. "What's all the whispering about? I don't want you snot-nose kids trying any big-time escapes."

I was going to mouth off and inform him that since we weren't exactly criminals (what can they do to you for a little speeding?), there was no reason for us to try to escape. But R. G. must have heard me take in air in preparation, because he poked me in the ribs.

"Let him have his fun," he whispered. "He hasn't felt so important since Len and Dooley put the cow in the girls' gym."

That had been a big day in Traxler's life. He'd evacuated the gym and cordoned off the area, bellowing instructions for all of us to stay behind a rope barrier. Then he crept into the gym, gun drawn. A couple minutes later, he triumphantly led out the bewildered cow while we all cheered. Some brilliant detective work, helped along by a little bribery, brought out the identity of the perpetrators, and Traxler tried, convicted, and punished Len and Dooley on the spot. He made them clean out the gym, which was pretty mucky since the cow had been in there over the weekend. Len and Dooley are town guys, and they're not used to that kind of thing. Cleaning up what the cow left made them barf, so they had to clean that up, too. Mr. Shafter, our music teacher, went around singing, "Let the punishment fit the crime," which he said was from a Gilbert and Sullivan opera.

Traxler had felt very pleased with himself.

Anyway, you could understand why Traxler had it in for teenagers. That was only *one* of the things that have happened.

"What's he going to do to us?" I whispered to R. G.

"I don't know, but I hope he lets Snyde share *your* cell and not mine." R. G.'s face was deadpan.

I knew he was teasing me. He didn't seem to be taking it all very seriously. But then, why should he? What did he have at stake? The guys on the school bus would probably think he was a hero for bugging Traxler. But I kept thinking about what Jordan thought, watching us being paraded past everybody in the police car. And how Susu would use it.

I wondered what Traxler would say if I told him he had probably ruined my chances of starting a career that could have led to the White House. Knowing Traxler, I imagine he would think he had saved his country from the disaster of a woman president.

When we got to the courthouse, Traxler pulled into the parking lot and stopped. Getting out of the car, he opened the back door and then just stood looking at us, his thumbs hooked over his gunbelt.

"Oughta throw you wise guys and that mutt in the slammer overnight," he growled. "Teach you not to mess with the law." He pulled a sigh up from somewhere down near the tops of his shiny boots. "But what the H, I'm a patient man. I'll let you go with a coupla warnings. Keep your noses clean, and *don't let me see that mutt around here again. Hear?*"

38

Snyde, who had been completely docile ever since we had got into the police car, raised his lip and showed Traxler a gleaming fang.

Traxler stepped back, putting his hand on his gun. "Maybe I'll keep the mutt here. Charge him with disturbing the peace yesterday and scaring that poor little girl out of her undies."

Poor little girl, my foot! But I held my tongue. All I said was, "It isn't Snyde's fault he's here today, Mr. Traxler. It's mine."

"Go home," Traxler said. "Go call your folks and have them come get you. And get that heap off the road out there on Indian Ridge. It's liable to cause an accident."

He heaved up another sigh. I figured it was meant to increase our sense of guilt. Either that or he had a fatal lung disease. He brought up a third gust when R. G. asked him for a dime to make the phone call. I wanted to tell R. G. we'd better get out of there before Traxler died on the spot and we were charged with contributing to his death.

R. G.'s dad came and got us in his pickup truck. We towed Belch back down to McCabe's shop and left it out in front.

On the way home, R. G.'s dad described how he would like to push that miserable bleep-bleep car over the bleep-bleep cliff into Bear River and be rid of the bleep-bleep thing.

But R. G. said he thought he knew what adjustments needed to be made. McCabe could do them tomorrow, and then it would run fine. I said I hoped so because something around there ought to run and it sure wasn't me, since my campaign was a disaster.

R. G.'s dad suggested that maybe my campaign needed a few adjustments, too. R. G. said that my campaign would

39

soon be running as good as Belch, which didn't give me any
confidence.

Frankly, if I had read my horoscope that morning, I
think it would have said to stay in bed.

Gloria and Blaine and Junior were there at our house visiting when Snyde and I got home. They come over almost
every Sunday night so Junior can transform us all into a
bunch of baby-talking idiots with that one-toothed grin of
his.

The enchantment session was well under way when
Snyde and I walked in. I decided it wasn't the time to announce that I'd recently been apprehended by the law.

"Look, Trish," Mom said, hanging onto Junior with
one arm while she ran a finger of the other hand across his
pink gums. "I think he's sprouting another tooth."

Junior gummed on Mom's finger, tasting it.

"Hi, kid," I said. I held out my arms and Junior came
into them with a happy gurgle. I wished it would be that
easy to attract Jordan.

I danced around the room while Junior giggled and
yelled his delight. He really is a special kid. Not that I'm
prejudiced or anything. But cute as he is, I'm always secretly
glad he's not mine. I mean, Gloria spends her entire time
taking care of him, and he's all she ever talks about any
more. She says she has everything she always wanted. That's
fine for her, but I wonder if a husband and babies and a
little house would be enough to make me think I had everything.

Then I thought about being married to Jordan and
having his-and-hers careers. He would be the governor of the
state and I would be a lawyer. (Or could it be that *I* would

be governor of the state and *he* would be a lawyer? I still had to find out how that would sit with him.) Anyway, I imagined us having this cute baby with Jordan's laser eyes, and I'd go off to the office every day, and I wouldn't be home to see the baby grow teeth and hear it say words for the first time. Was that what I wanted?

I didn't know *what* I wanted.

"Hey, Trish," Blaine said, "I hear you're going to be our lady executive. Trish Harker, Girl President."

"I'm running, Blaine." I stopped dancing and wiggled my fingers in front of Junior's eyes. He laughed and grabbed for them. "That doesn't mean I'm going to win, though."

"My brother thinks it's in the bag."

I might have known R. G. would talk to him about me. "Oh? Why does he think that?"

Blaine shrugged. "He says you've got it all—beauty, brains, speaking ability, and the guts to slug it out with a tough opponent."

I didn't know R. G. thought all those things about me. "You're putting me on," I told Blaine.

Blaine held up his right hand. "Swear to God. He said every word. Didn't he, Gloria?"

Gloria looked up from the jar of baby food she was warming for Junior. "He sure did. He says you're going to be junior-class president and then Associated Student Body president the next year. And he's going to be behind you every step of the way."

Blaine grinned at Gloria. "I'm glad you never had any notions about being president of anything, sugar."

Gloria looked at him with what I used to call her "moo-cow eyes." "Why not, lover?"

Blaine walked over and patted her fanny. "I'd rather

see my woman holding a cook pot than a gavel any day. I just want you always to be my little homecoming queen, sweetie."

Gloria smiled as if he had paid her a compliment. Turning her head, she kissed him over her shoulder. "Whatever you want, darlin'," she said. "You're the boss."

I had a vision of Gloria dancing like a puppet at the end of strings held by Blaine.

But then the picture changed. *I* was the puppet and R. G. held the strings.

Just what was it with R. G., anyway? Why did he want me to go for these presidential offices? What was in it for him? Would he be mad if I asked him?

After Gloria and her family left, I told Mom and Dad about the run-in with Traxler.

"You're lucky he didn't give you a ticket for speeding." Dad had the Sunday paper spread out on the kitchen table and was catching up on what he hadn't read before his nap.

"We weren't really speeding," I objected. "R. G. was just trying to build up enough speed to get Belch over Indian Ridge without stalling."

"I imagine Mr. Traxler understood that," Mom said. "Which is probably why he *didn't* give you a ticket." She was sitting at the kitchen table, too, working on her genealogy sheets.

"But," I persisted, "we were outside his jurisdiction when he picked us up."

Dad tipped his head back and looked at me through his bifocals. "He's allowed to go outside his jurisdiction when he's in hot pursuit, which I take it he was. What is it you're so fired up about, Trish? He did you a favor. If he hadn't picked you up, you and R. G. would probably still be sitting there in that dead car."

He was right, of course. But just then I could have used a little sympathy and a couple of nasty remarks about Traxler. I should have known I wouldn't get the remarks from Mom and Dad. Whenever any of us kids have had run-ins with teachers or police or anybody in authority like that, Mom and Dad have made us examine the situation to see both sides.

To be fair, it wasn't Traxler's fault that Jordan and Susu and the others had seen us in his car. But still, it was *because* of him that we'd been seen.

And maybe recorded on Riley's film.

I decided to call R. G. After the *hello*'s and *how are you*'s, I asked if he had talked to Riley yet.

"About what?" He sounded surprised.

Sometimes R. G. could be so dense. "About the picture he took, of course. Maybe we can outbid Susu."

"Trish, Riley would nick us a bundle for it, if it's a good clear photo. I've decided it's not worth it."

He had decided. *He* wasn't the one whose whole future was at stake.

"R. G." I tried to keep my voice calm. "Susu could make a big thing about us being hauled around in Traxler's black-and-white. She'll do a number on me just the way she did on Arlene McKenna. All the kids will be laughing their heads off at me. I won't get a single vote."

"You'll always get *my* vote, Trish," R. G. said. When I started to sputter he went on, "How can we stop Susu? She didn't have any photos of Arlene, but she managed just fine without them. Susu's pretty creative when it comes to smearing people. She doesn't need photographs."

Everybody was so confounded reasonable. First Mom and Dad, and now R. G. Was that a quality that was doled out only to other people? Was that why R. G. was in control of *my* campaign?

My grip on the telephone tightened. "I'm going to do something about it even if you aren't. I'll call Riley and offer him double what Susu will pay. I'll call Susu and tell her how unfair it would be to use what happened today."

There was a short silence during which I listened to the line hum and wondered if I was really as hysterical as I sounded to my own ears.

"Okay," R. G. finally said. "It's up to you, Trish. But think about it first. That picture isn't going to make the difference in whether you win or lose."

"Okay, R. G., I'll think about it." I bit off the words. "I'll tell you tomorrow what I decide to do."

"Trish. . . ."

I thought R. G. was going to say more. I waited while the line hummed again. But all he said was, "I'll see you tomorrow."

He knew I wouldn't call either Riley or Susu. He knew I'd figure out that if Riley knew how much I wanted the picture, the price would triple and that if I started begging Susu, she would know she had the upper hand.

He knew I would follow his advice. Dance, puppet, dance. Gloria was Blaine's little homecoming queen and I was R. G.'s little presidential candidate.

When I went out to help Dad with the chores, Mrs. Toomey was heading for her chicken coop. "Though deep'ning trials come your way," she sang, "press on, press on, ye saints of God. . . ."

It was that kind of a day, all right.

44

5

I SEMI-EXPECTED SUSU TO HAVE COPIES of the picture Riley had taken plastered all over the school on Monday morning. I was really relieved to see the campus looking as drab as usual.

"Maybe Susu realized how mean it would be to use it," I said hopefully.

Dannalee snorted. "If she *has* realized how mean it would be, she'll use it without a doubt. Just be prepared." Dannalee was wearing something that looked like a fishnet draped over her jeans and shirt. That kind of thing would make most people look a little demented, but it just made her look artsy-craftsy, which is the way Dannalee is.

R. G. agreed with Dannalee. "Just keep your cool, Trish. Susu's going to be pitching all kinds of things your way. Don't let it throw you."

R. G. had acted relieved when I told him on the bus that I hadn't made any phone calls. He had blown a blast on his tuba that had got the attention of everyone, even

Lester, the bus driver. Then he had made a little speech about the next president of the junior class being right there on the Wolf Creek bus in full, living color. It had been a little embarrassing, but fun.

In spite of Dannalee's and R. G.'s warnings, I relaxed when I didn't see any evidence of Susu's dirty work. But that lasted only as far as my first-period English class. When I walked in there, the first thing I saw was a big cartoon drawing of Snyde and me. Underneath was written "Harker and Barker."

It wasn't an action cartoon. I mean, it was just our heads with big, dumb, Orphan Annie eyes staring vacantly out at the class. There was no mistaking that it was Snyde and me, though. The cartoonist had drawn Snyde's George Washington face so that anybody who had ever seen him would know who it was. And there was no way the other face, with the freckles across the nose and the big front teeth, could be anybody's but mine.

So much for Marv and his ideas of defusing Susu.

There were a lot of remarks when I came in. Some of them were from kids I didn't think had ever noticed me before. Remembering R. G.'s advice, I just smiled and waved, obedient little candidate that I was.

"Hey, Harker," somebody said, "I hear you really chewed up Susu on Saturday."

"No, that was her Barker," somebody else said.

"She chewed up her Barker?" Everybody laughed.

The jokes went on and I continued to smile.

By the end of the day, the smile had almost become a grimace. My cheeks ached, and so did my head.

"How'd it go?" R. G. asked, plopping down beside me

on the bus. He balanced his tuba on his knees as if he intended to stay.

I told him about the cartoon.

R. G. nodded. "There were ones like it in several of the first-period classrooms that have mostly sophomores. I think we'll get the next installment tomorrow."

"You mean there'll be more?" My mouth hung open as I stared at R. G.

"Count on it. Susu can't start the campaigning yet, so she's doing the next best thing."

I groaned and stared glumly out of the window. Dannalee was heading toward the bus at a trot. Her fishnet had shifted a little during the day, and a piece of it was dragging the ground behind her.

"Maybe I could just paint a smile on my face, like a clown's," I said, turning back to R. G.

"Wouldn't be a bad idea." He grinned at me, but there was sympathy in his brown eyes.

Dannalee burst into the bus like an exploding firecracker. "Great gobs of gooey gumballs!" she exclaimed. "Wait'll I tell you what I just heard."

Flopping down on the seat in front of R. G. and me, she leaned over the back of it and said, "Blair Bates told me that Sheila Moss told him that Glen Daley told her that Amelia Slade told him that Jordan said it, so it came straight from the horse's mouth."

"More or less," R. G. said.

Dannalee stared at him. "What do you mean by that?"

"Straight from the horse's mouth but filtered through several sets of ears and interpreted by a few interim minds," R. G. said.

"Speak English," Dannalee told him, then leaned close again. "This will knock you off your pins," she whispered.

Dannalee likes to build up suspense. "What, what, what?" I begged.

Dannalee looked around at all the other kids who were shifting a little closer to hear. "Tell you later," she said. "Emergency session, right after school. We'll meet at your house, Trish." She rolled her eyes and twitched her head toward the other kids. "There may be spies," she whispered.

There was no use trying to get more out of her, so we changed the subject. R. G. stayed there beside me, which was about the first time that year a guy had broken the unwritten rule that guys sat in the back of the bus and girls in the front.

As soon as I got home, I asked Mom if there were any leftovers from Sunday dinner.

"Why?" she asked. "Is the Hoover coming over?"

"The Hoover" is Mom's nickname for R. G., because he always vacuums up any available food when he comes to our house. R. G.'s mother died three years ago and just he and his dad are at home now. R. G. does most of the meal-fixing, and he's very good at it. But he really appreciates my mom's cooking. He says his stomach flashes a vacancy sign whenever he heads in our direction.

I dropped my books on the dining-room table and followed Mom into the kitchen, where she started sawing thicks slabs of her famous homemade bread.

"Put everything out," she said. "That way he won't have to look in the refrigerator, and our Jell-O salad for supper will be safe."

Mom loves to feed R. G., but she plays this game that

she has to defend the family food from him practically at gunpoint.

I pulled the leftover roast beef from the refrigerator, along with pickles, mayonnaise, mustard, and the lettuce and tomatoes Marv had bought in Pratt on Saturday. I carried everything to the kitchen table and shoved aside the family genealogy sheets that Mom works on whenever she has time. She has pages and pages of the names and birthdates of our dead ancestors. Some of the family lines she has traced back into the sixteenth and seventeenth centuries. It really depresses me to look at those charts. It makes me think that people are born just to grow up and produce more people so *they* can grow up and produce *more* people. All you end up as is a name on a chart.

Or a picture in a yearbook with a blank space underneath.

Through the kitchen window I could see R. G. marching across the fields playing his tuba as if he were a one-man Fourth of July parade or something. Tucked under one armpit he carried something that looked like a grocery bag.

Dannalee arrived just then on her bicycle, and she, R. G., and Snyde, who had announced their arrival, came in together. They greeted Mom with a "Hi, Mrs. Harker," and a couple of barks. R. G. was the one who barked. Snyde just wagged his tail.

"How'd you know I was hungry?" R. G.'s eyes zeroed in on the food as he put his tuba and the paper bag on a chair.

"Just a lucky guess," Mom said. "Go ahead and build your own."

We told Mom about what had happened in school that day as R. G. constructed sandwiches for himself, Dannalee,

49

and me. He stacked up all the ingredients and mortared them with mayonnaise while he gave his opinion as to what Susu was up to.

"The election rules say that posters can't be put up until the first day of campaign week," he said. "So I think Susu is going to lay a little groundwork with the cartoons. Probably draw a new cartoon each day this week." Scraping together a mound of scraps, R. G. dropped them into Snyde's drooling cavern. Snyde swallowed them and drooled for more.

"Maybe we should figure out some way to get back at her," Dannalee suggested. "I could draw her face on those cartoons with daggers shooting out of her big fat mouth."

R. G. unhinged his jaws, took a bite of his sandwich, and chewed a moment before answering. "I figure she's doing this for two reasons," he said. "One, she saw a good opportunity to tear you down a little. And two, she's using it as a diversionary tactic. She *wants* to draw our fire her way. That way we're concentrating on her rather than on Jordan."

"Good thinking," Mom said.

R. G. grinned modestly. "I've been reading about the Civil War. I've learned a lot that we can use in this battle."

"I'm glad Trish has you on her side," Mom said. "Maybe you can zap Pratt High into the 1980's with a girl class president."

"All I need is a guy to tell me what to do," I said, feeling mean all of a sudden.

R. G. blinked as he looked at me in surprise. His jaws stopped working, but he didn't say anything.

"That isn't what I meant," Mom said. "That's 1950's talk. I meant that you can use good ideas from whatever source."

"I'm sorry," I said. "I guess I'm just getting nervous

about this whole thing. Let's go upstairs and get down to making some plans for this circus. Maybe I'll feel better when we've figured out what we're going to do."

"Speaking of circus," Dannalee said, gathering up her sandwich, "wait'll I tell you what Blair Bates told me that Sheila Moss told him that. . . ."

"Well, let's hear it." I herded the two of them up the stairs to my room. The three of us had been meeting there since we were little kids.

R. G. brought his paper bag with him, and Dannalee asked what was in it.

"I'll show you after you tell us what Blair Bates told you that Sheila Moss told him, et cetera, et cetera, et cetera." R. G. held the bag in the air with one hand when Dannalee snatched at it.

"I'll never be able to concentrate until I find out what's so mysterious in that dumb sack," Dannalee said.

R. G. shrugged. "Okay. I'll show you."

Putting the uneaten half of his sandwich on my dresser, he upended the bag on my bed, dumping out a woman's red-and-green-flowered dress. "It's part of my Tootsie Day costume. I thought I'd show it to the two of you and see if it's okay."

We were having our first annual Tootsie Day on Wednesday, and it was getting mixed reactions. The guys were supposed to dress like girls and the girls like guys. Some of the kids thought it was corny. Others liked the idea. Evidently R. G. was going along with it. Personally, I thought it sounded fun.

"Try it on, R. G.," I said. "It's hard to tell what it looks like without you in it."

I thought R. G. would go into Marv's bedroom to put

on his costume. But he shucked off his plaid shirt right there in front of Dannalee and me. Not that we hadn't seen his bare chest before. After all our swimming parties over on the river, we certainly knew what his chest looked like. But it seemed a little different there in my bedroom.

It wasn't a bad-looking chest, as chests go. It was hairless, but R. G. works hard on his dad's farm so his arms and body are firm and well-muscled. I'm not hung up on chests or anything, but I do like a guy to look substantial. I know a couple of guys who look as if they've had their rib cages amputated. I always thought being hugged by a guy like that would be like standing against an open window.

Watching R. G. struggle to pull the flowered dress down over his head, I caught myself wondering what it would be like to be hugged against his firm chest.

What was the matter with me? How come I was getting turned on by a chest all of a sudden—and R. G.'s, at that? I was mad at R. G., wasn't I? Or was I? Why should I be mad at him just because he was doing his best to help me run a good campaign? And the better my campaign was, the more dazzled Jordan would be.

I shifted my eyes from R. G.'s chest to Dannalee, who, I saw, was also regarding him with interest.

"Are you going to wear a bra, R. G.?" she asked. Her thoughts were obviously quite different from mine. "I've got one that's padded. We could stuff it with toilet paper."

R. G. was struggling with the dress. His head popped through its neck, and he peered at us like a disoriented turtle. "What am I doing wrong?" he asked. "I can't seem to get into this thing."

Dannalee walked over to him. "You forgot to undo the zipper, dumbbell." She giggled as she made the necessary adjustments and helped R. G. pull the dress down over his jeans.

It was a familiar dress. R. G.'s mother had worn it a lot when she was alive. I wondered if he was thinking of that as he looked at himself in the mirror.

"Fits okay," he said. He looked down at his flat front. "Except there. Do you really think I should wear a bra?"

Dannalee nodded. "Did Dustin Hoffman have an ironed-out chest in *Tootsie?*"

"Okay," R. G. agreed. "I'll see if I can coax Belch over to your house to pick it up later."

"You look smashing," I said. "Lester will probably pinch you when you get on the school bus Wednesday."

Lester, our bus driver, was kind of a barometer for us girls, indicating the state of our appearance. If his eyebrows went up, it meant we looked classy. If he groaned, we knew it was dog day. When we wore something Lester considered too tight or too short or too low-cut or otherwise suggestive, he tried to pinch us as we passed his driver's seat. Other than that, he was a very good driver, patient and careful, so nobody ever complained too much.

R. G. grinned as he yanked the dress off over his head. "I wish he *would* pinch me," he said. "I'd likely break his fingers."

"Oh, come on," Dannalee said. "He's harmless. He just thinks he's funny."

"And he'll keep pinching you as long as you let him think he's funny." R. G. folded the dress and stuffed it into the paper bag again. "Why don't you tell him sometimes to keep his grubby hands off you?"

To tell the truth, it *did* make me feel grungy to have Lester tweak my bottom. But I was kind of amazed that

R. G. understood. Most of the other guys laughed like crazy when Lester pinched a girl.

R. G. put his shirt on, buttoning it up as he went to the chair next to my dresser and plopped down. That was his usual seat when the three of us were in my room. Dannalee and I always sat on the bed.

I sat there now, looking at R. G. and wondering what it would be like if he came over and sat beside me on the bed. Mentally I erased Dannalee, since I wouldn't want her to see anything like that. Then I thought of him pulling me close, and maybe I would put my hands inside his shirt and run them across the hard muscles of his chest.

"Okay," R. G. said, "back to business. It's your turn, Dannalee. Tell us what Blair Bates said that Sheila Moss told him and all that."

"You'll *die*," Dannalee said.

I turned off my thoughts of making out with R. G. How could I sit there thinking things like that when I had a campaign to plan? A campaign that was going to make me look good to Jordan. Jordan with his laser eyes and sculptured mouth. I wondered what *his* chest was like.

What kind of a sex-crazed female was I turning into?

"My sandwich is gone," R. G. said. "Snyde got it while I was trying on the dress."

I hadn't even heard Snyde come in. But he was over by my closet, licking the last telltale crumb from the floor.

And that's the way Susu was going to steal the election, if I didn't watch out. While I sat around thinking about guys' chests, she was going to sneak in and carry off the whole sandwich. I wouldn't even have made a good start.

Then what would Jordan think of me?

6

"WELL." DANNALEE PUT THE LAST BITE of her sandwich in her mouth and dusted her hands together. "This is what I heard." She chewed a few times, just to build suspense. "Blair Bates told me—"

"We know the history of the information," I said. "Just tell us."

"Well." Dannalee swallowed. "Jordan is going to have a campaign like something right out of the movies. You know how we always have a parade of candidates on the opening day of the campaign? Well, Jordan's going to have a parade all his own. He's talked a lot of the marching band kids into performing while some of his guys haul him around the campus on a little platform they're building. He'll call it his 'campaign platform.' Nobody else has *ever* done anything like that."

"Wow," I breathed. "I wonder how he'll top that next year when he runs for ASB president." I was filled with admiration for Jordan. He *would* think of something spectacular.

R. G. leaned back against my dresser. "He won't have to top it. If he wins this one, he can coast into that one. He figures no one will dare run against him after this year's show."

"I don't know if *I* dare run against him this year," I said, "unless we can do something that will make me look as exciting as he is."

"Hey, how about this?" Dannalee sat up straight, her eyes sparkling. "I heard once about this lady who made her living toe-dancing on the back of a pig. *That* would get everybody's attention."

R. G. laughed. "I'll supply the pig."

"Maybe I could use two pigs," I said, "and leap from one to the other. Come on, Dannalee. Be serious."

Dannalee shrugged. "Okay, so maybe it's not the best idea. It had an unhappy ending, anyway. The lady slipped off the pig's back one day and broke her leg. Then she couldn't dance and make money, so she had to eat the pig."

"You're making that up, Dannalee."

"I read it somewhere."

"Sure."

"Well, we have to think unusual if we're going to top Jordan."

R. G. rubbed his chin. There was a nick in it and I wondered if he'd tried shaving.

"We don't need to top Jordan," he said. "We'll just run a low-key campaign and concentrate on the issues."

"What *are* the issues?" I hadn't thought much about issues.

"Whatever we decide they'll be. Funding for the prom. More preparation for the PSATs. Getting rid of the mystery meat in the cafeteria. Whatever. But we *could* use a gimmick of some kind."

Gimmick. I thought of the treaure hunt in the hymnbook on Sunday. I told R. G. and Dannalee about it. "Maybe we could use that idea somehow. Everybody likes a treasure hunt. Maybe I could have a secret campaign promise that I would reveal at the assembly. The posters during the week could give clues."

"What will your secret campaign promise be?" Dannalee asked.

"I don't know. We'll have to figure out something big."

There was a moment of silence. Snyde filled it with loud snaps of his teeth as he went after a flea on his back.

"So maybe it's *not* such a good idea," I said.

"It's a great idea," R. G. said. "I was just thinking of the possibilities. We could make big paper footprints leading from one clue to the next and write 'A vote for Trish is a step in the right direction' on them." Putting two fingers between the buttons of his shirt, he scratched at his chest.

"Chest," I said, thinking again how I'd like to run my hands over R. G.'s smooth chest.

Dannalee and R. G. looked at me, puzzled.

"*Treasure* chest," I said. "We'll have a locked treasure chest with my secret campaign promise inside. We'll open it and reveal the promise at the assembly."

Dannalee clapped her hands. "Hey, we're rolling. I'm already getting ideas for posters."

"Okay, here's how we'll set things up for Monday." R. G. got up to prowl around my room while he spoke. "We're going to use mystery. Suspense. Intrigue. Let Susu hack at you all she wants, Trish. We'll outdo her and Jordan with adventure."

Hey, whose idea was it anyway? How come R. G. was yanking the strings again?

But as R. G. outlined his plan, I had to admit it sounded good. What could I do but go along with it?

Nothing much happened the next day except that there was a new cartoon on the chalkboards in the sophomore classrooms. This time the drawing of me had a hand up to its ear. Underneath it said,

> "Hark.
> Someone's near.
> Bark, my faithful barker, dear,
> Bark and snarl and fierce appear,
> Fill that person full of fear.
> Hark."

Snyde's drawing had fangs and a dripping tongue.

Our English teacher, Ms. Evans, eyed the cartoon and read the poem aloud before she erased it.

"I wish," she said, "that you people showed this much creativity in your assignments."

I spent another day smiling and playing it cool, according to R. G.'s instructions. He said on the bus that he was making a flow chart to help us get everything going the next week. He said he'd have it ready when he and Dannalee and I got together again the next afternoon.

Wednesday was Tootsie Day. I decided to wear Marv's cowboy boots, a pair of his jeans, a fringed buckskin shirt, and his big ten-gallon hat. When I got on the bus, I wished

I hadn't worn a costume, because not many of the other people were in costume. Some of them carried paper bags and said they would change when they got to school. Ann Hart said she was going to wait and see if the town kids came in costume before she changed. That's when I began to worry. What if only R. G., Dannalee, and I showed up in costumes? We'd really look like a trio of hicks. What would Susu do with that? I hoped R. G. had changed his mind about wearing that dress.

But he hadn't. He came loping toward the bus wearing not only the dress but also, judging from his shape, Danna-lee's bra. A red shoulder purse flapped against his hip. He wore his own shoes, but in one hand he carried a pair of high-heeled white sandals. In the other he carried his tuba. On his head, a frowsy black wig roosted like an uneasy crow.

An orchestra of whistles struck up as he boarded the bus.

"Gawd-a-mighty," Lester said. "Who's this vision of loveliness?" He reached out to pinch R. G. "Whatcha doin' tonight, honey-baby?"

"I'm going out for my karate lesson, snookums," R. G. said sweetly as he caught Lester's reaching hand in the bell of his tuba. Giving it a twist, he brought Lester right up out of his seat, yelping with pain.

"You better not mess with us women of the eighties, lover," R. G. said, and then grinned back at the other guys. "Hey, you turkeys, where are your dresses?"

Lester retrieved his hand from the tuba and shook it. "You coulda broke it," he said.

"Maybe you better keep it where it belongs then, sugarbuns," R. G. said. "Get your jollies some other way."

All of the girls cheered as R. G. made his way down the aisle.

Lester put the bus in gear, and then turned his face around. "Why'n hell didn't you tell me you didn't like it?" He managed a grin. "Even an old lecher can take a hint if he's hit on the head with it."

"Forget it, Lester," I said. "Just let your fingers do their walking in the Yellow Pages from now on."

The bus started rolling again, with Lester muttering something about ruining a guy's fun. I got the idea he wouldn't be touching any of us girls again. I wondered why none of us had ever slapped him down. Where had we got the idea that we had to go along with that kind of thing?

"I don't know," Dannalee said when she got on and I asked her the same thing. "I guess we figured the guys wouldn't like us if we didn't." She was wearing a Charlie Chaplin suit.

"But that's like the world my mom grew up in," I said.

Dannalee shrugged. "Some things don't change." She turned around and made a "good work" sign to R. G. with a thumb and forefinger. Turning back to me, she said, "Maybe we should check out those chicks back there."

I looked. R. G. was talking the other guys into putting on their costumes. Gordie Coons was pulling a tube-top sundress over his paunchy front. Todd Miller wore a polyester pantsuit. Dave Jensen's dress showed his hairy chest. They were walking around back there, twitching their fannies and talking in high voices. I couldn't help but laugh.

Riley McQuaid was lurking with his camera in the bus-unloading area when we got there. I figured he'd been hired by Susu to get more embarrassing pictures in case I showed up looking ridiculous that day. But he didn't get any pictures. All of the Wolf Creek kids closed in around R. G. and Dannalee and me and escorted us right to the front door of the high school. It wasn't until that moment that I realized I might have the start of a power base, right there with the kids who rode the bus with me each day.

I didn't have long to enjoy that thought, though. I was heading for my English class to see what new cartoon awaited me when a guy named Sam caught up with me. He lives on the other side of Pratt and walks down Main Street on his way to school.

"You won't believe what's in the front window of Anderson's Photography Shop," he panted.

"I'll believe anything," I said. "What is it?"

Sam rolled his eyes. "Go see." He took off for his first-period class.

At least it gave me something else to think about besides the cartoon, which that day was a drawing of both Snyde and me with open mouths showing fangs. Underneath it said, "Her bite is worse than her Barker."

I didn't see R. G. until the Tootsie Day judging on the quad at noon. All the people who had worn costumes were supposed to line up there and be judged. I found him in the lineup, teetering around on the high-heeled sandals he had brought.

"I think I know what Susu did with the picture of us in Traxler's black-and-white," I said.

"I know I know what she did with it," R. G. said. "Or rather, what she got Riley to do with it. About seven guys have already told me. They've been asking me when I got out of jail."

I had been kind of hoping I was wrong about it being

the picture in Anderson's Photography Shop. But there was no way I could be, not when Riley worked there part-time.

I sighed. "We might as well go see how bad it is. Maybe we can walk uptown after the judging."

"We can go right now, as far as I'm concerned." R. G. twitched his bra strap and shrugged his shoulders, trying to get comfortable. "I don't know how girls wear these things all the time. I feel like I'm in a harness."

I didn't want to talk about bras with R. G. It kind of embarrassed me. I couldn't even tell him that his "bosom" seemed to have slipped a little. It was way up on his chest, even with his armpits.

"Let's stay here for a while," I said. "You might win a prize."

I didn't really care whether R. G. won a prize, but I had just seen Jordan. He was acting as master of ceremonies, dressed in white pants, a red-and-white-striped jacket, and a dark blue tie.

"Hi, Trish," he called when he saw me. "Great costume."

Melting, I watched him climb up on the platform that had been set up on the quad. He had a bullhorn in his hand, which he put up to his mouth.

"Everybody stay in line," he said. "Let the judges look you over. We have some super prizes to give out for the best costumes."

"Where's yours?" somebody yelled from the audience.

He looked down at his bright, fresh jacket that really made the flowered dresses the other guys wore look tacky. "Sorry about this, folks. Had to do a little demo in my government class this morning. What can I say?"

"Say you'll wear one of your mother's dresses next year," someone said.

Jordan's mother is Emily Avery, attorney-at-law. She's about half Jordan's size, and she wears these little tiny size-five dresses. But Jordan always says she's packed with dynamite.

"I'll do it," Jordan said into the bullhorn. "Maybe I'll even wear *two* of them." He laughed, and that changed his ordinary face into something any girl would vote for. "Now," he said, "let's get on with the judging."

R. G. won a prize, and so did Dannalee for her Charlie Chaplin costume. The prizes weren't anything to breathe hard about. R. G. won a free manicure at Ethel's Beauty Salon. Dannalee won a free tire-change at McCabe's Auto Shop, which she gave to R. G. since she doesn't have a car. Manny Lopez, who wore a sequined red dress, won a lipstick from Johnson's Drugstore. Other kids won cones from the Dairy Freeze.

We didn't have much time left after the judging, so R. G. didn't bother to change his sandals before he, Dannalee, and I started uptown to look in the Anderson's Photography Shop window. We only had to go four blocks, so he thought he could make it all right. In the high heels, he clumped alongside Dannalee and me like a herd of mules.

Most of the people we met along the street smiled when they saw us. A couple of older women whispered behind their hands, and one sunburned old farmer said, "What the hell's happened to the world these days?"

I guess we didn't exactly look like a trio of all-American high school students. Marv's big boots were rubbing my feet a lot, so I walked spraddle-legged to avoid some of the pain.

Dannalee's mascara mustache was running a little as she began to sweat in the warm sun. R. G.'s wig was hanging on one side of his head, and he had yanked his bosom down around his waist.

But we wanted to see that picture.

It was there, all right, blown up so that it practically filled the window. There were some other pictures in the display, too, but who could see any of them?

The photo was very clear. Our faces, R. G.'s and mine, looked out from the inside of Traxler's car. Our eyes were squinted and our mouths looked tight. Snyde's dog face between us gave the whole thing kind of a sinister appearance. The back of Traxler's head looked authoritative and righteous.

"Wow," Dannalee breathed. "What did you guys *do*?"

"Hey," I said, "if *you* react that way, what are the people who don't know us so well going to think?"

"Maybe we can talk Mr. Anderson into taking it out of the window," R. G. suggested. He clumped into the store with Dannalee and me right behind him.

"You kids trick or treating?" Mr. Anderson asked from behind the counter.

R. G. explained why we were in costume, and then why we had come into the store.

Mr. Anderson nodded when R. G. finished. "That Riley is a fine worker, but he does get a mite frisky sometimes. I'll tell him to get that picture out of the window when he comes this afternoon. I'd do it myself, but I'm not spry enough to crawl up in there any more."

"I'll do it," R. G. offered.

Mr. Anderson showed him how to crawl through a little door that led into the window display. R. G. got in there all right, but when he reached for the picture, he turned his ankle on his high heels. He pitched across the window area and ricocheted off the wall. The whole display tumbled down. R. G. danced across the scattered pictures, his arms windmilling for balance. Every time his big feet came down on those three-inch spikes attached to his heels, he shot forward again, repeating the whole routine.

That's when Traxler came.

He stood there in front of the display window, his eyes sliding from R. G.'s crow wig to his hairy bare legs. Turning his face to the sky, he put up his arms.

"You can take me anytime, God," he said. "I've seen everything now."

We had to promise Traxler that we would confine our delinquencies to Wolf Creek before he would let us go. The editor of the *Pratt Bugle*, whose office is across the street from Anderson's, ambled over. He said he would just report the facts.

"A wipeout," I said as we hurried back to school, late for our afternoon classes. "Who's going to vote for me now?" Worse still, Jordan wasn't going to endanger his career by ever being seen with a girl who seemed to be speeding headlong toward a criminal record.

R. G. grinned. His lipstick was smeared all over his chin. His shape had lumps where no lumps ought to be. He had taken off his wig, and his hair stood up in all directions.

"At least we've got this thing." He held up the picture. "It could be worse."

I didn't believe that then.

7

ON THURSDAY, R. G., DANNALEE, AND I decided we'd better meet somewhere after school and get a start on our posters.

"Give me time to feed my pigs, then I'll fix some supper for all of us," R. G. said.

I decided to go home with Dannalee so I could help her haul all her art stuff to R. G.'s.

Dannalee's mother was ironing a manuscript when we got to their house. She sends her romances out so many times that they get pretty wrinkled. She irons them before she sends them out again.

"Another rejection, Mom?" Dannalee walked over and gave her mom a peck on the cheek.

"My lands," Mrs. Davis said, looking up from the ironing board. "I didn't hear you coming, Danni. Hi, Trish."

"Why?" Dannalee asked. "Where were you this time? Morocco? Paris? Shanghai?"

"South Africa," Mrs. Davis said. "I spent the whole afternoon in a diamond mine near Johannesburg. And to answer your first question, yes, I did get this manuscript back today. It's *Lips of Flame*. You probably remember it."

"Sure." Dannalee opened the refrigerator door and peered inside. "That's the one about the girl who was going to be sacrificed to a volcano."

Mrs. David nodded. "And she was saved by a helicopter pilot who turned out to be a rich dentist."

"So what is this South Africa one about?" Dannalee was having a hard time finding anything in the refrigerator. Mrs. Davis doesn't keep tons of stuff around to eat like my mom does.

"You read part of it, Danni. Remember?" Mrs. Davis' eyes sparkled as she pressed the manuscript pages with the hot iron. "It's the one about Florinda."

Dannalee fished a jar of pickles and a plastic bag containing two heels of bread from the refrigerator. "Oh, yeah, I remember. She's the girl who falls in love with the handsome diamond thief."

"But he's not really a diamond thief," Mrs. Davis said. "Actually he owns the mine and is very rich. But Florinda doesn't know that. She won't find out until he rescues her from the real villain."

Mrs. Davis' romances are always exciting. Some girl is always getting into big trouble and being rescued by a handsome and rich man. Dannalee and I can't figure out why she has never been able to sell any of them.

"Has Luke kissed Florinda yet?" Dannalee asked. "That's always the best part."

Mrs. Davis put her iron down. "That's the chapter I wrote today. Want to test it out?"

"Sure," Dannalee and I said together.

Mrs. Davis uses Dannalee and me as thermometers. She

says if she can feel good about letting us read her stories, she hasn't made them too hot. If we like them, then they aren't too cool. Dannalee and I are always hoping she will get carried away and write something really steamy, but she says she doesn't do "bodice rippers." She says she would be embarrassed to let people know she sat around all day thinking about things like that.

"It's out on the washer." Mrs. Davis was heading for the little service porch that she uses as a writing room when Dannalee's father came into the house.

"Hope that's one of my shirts you've been squashing." He pointed toward the ironing board.

Mrs. Davis walked back to the board and held up a page of her manuscript. "It's just one of my stories. But I'll iron a shirt first thing in the morning. Are you all out of ironed shirts?"

Mr. Davis addressed the geranium on the windowsill. "She asks me if I'm all out of shirts. I haven't had an ironed shirt since Dannalee was a baby, and she asks me if I'm all out."

"I'll get to it," Mrs. Davis promised. "One of these days I'll iron them all before you have to wear them."

"What the hell, the cows don't care if my shirts are ironed," Mr. Davis said. "How you doing, Trish? Hey, how's about one of you women whomping me up a bite to eat? I'm taking the tractor over to Bill Pickett's place to see if he can figger out what's wrong with the thing. I think it needs a bunch of new parts, and I'm strapped for cash." He sighed. "I'll be late for supper, and my stomach's already setting up a holler."

Mrs. Davis opened the refrigerator door. "Oh, Harry,

I'm afraid we're all out of bread. I'm going to make biscuits for supper. The kind you like."

Mr. Davis squinted at the empty shelves, then looked down at his middle. "Might as well shrivel, stomach. There's nothing coming your way."

Dannalee giggled and held up the two heels of bread she had planned as a snack for us. "I'll make you a sandwich, Dad," she said. "Mom's been in South Africa all day. She can't make bread when she's romancing."

"Hell of a note," Mr. Davis grumbled. "I'm the only feller in town who starves to death while his wife's off kissing up a storm with some millionaire. Too bad you have to come back to this poor farmer every day, Norma."

Dannalee was searching a cupboard, where she found a can of Spam. "You'll be a rich businessman when Mom's romances start selling."

"I'll be president of the U. S. when hens have teeth, too," Mr. Davis muttered.

Mrs. Davis looked embarrassed. I wondered if it was because I was there or if she felt bad about what her husband was saying.

"I'm sorry, Harry," she said. "I should have made some bread yesterday. I just didn't get around to it." She looked toward his middle and cupped her hands around her mouth. "I'm sorry, stomach," she called.

"It's okay, Norma." Mr. Davis pulled her roughly against him. "I don't mind if you fool around on the typewriter. I just wish you'd take ahold and do the important things first."

"I'll try, Harry. I really will." Mrs. Davis gave him a quick kiss, then gathered up her freshly ironed manuscript.

I had felt sorry sometimes for Dannalee and Mr. Davis.

It was nice to have a mom who seemed to like nothing better than seeing that we were all comfortable and well fed. I had always felt that Mrs. Davis ought to "take ahold and do the important things first." But this time, for some reason, I thought of all the poems she had written for Dannalee and me to say. I thought of the plays she had written for our school classes to perform. I thought of the skits she had written for the neighborhood kids to do, and the stage she had helped us build under the tall cedars by their root cellar. I had made my first speech in front of an audience there, which meant that it was because of Mrs. Davis that I was running now for class president, sort of.

So what *were* the important things?

I was glad when Dannalee finished making the Spam sandwich for her father so we could go.

We found Mrs. Davis' latest chapter on the washing machine, as she had said. She kept her battered typewriter on a little utility table next to the washer. It was almost buried under unwashed laundry, but her stacks of typing paper and manuscripts were neat and orderly.

"Let's just take the kissy part," Dannalee said. She flipped through the pages, pulling out half a dozen.

We went up to Dannalee's room, where she flopped down on her bed. Patting the spot next to her she said, "We'll figure out what we have to take to R. G.'s after we read the romance."

Of course. Letting those pages lie around while we did something else would have been like having a big piece of chocolate cake right beside your mouth when you're dying to grub it up.

I stretched out beside Dannalee as she ran a finger down

the top page. "Here it is." She began reading in a breathy voice.

"He was looking down at her, and
Florinda knew that look. She was about
to be kissed.
"Something close to fear choked her
voice so she couldn't protest. His
overwhelming masculinity swept those
protests away. His powerful arms pulled
her close to his rock-hard chest.
"But he was a thief. A diamond thief.
How could she kiss a thief?"

Dannalee paused to take a bite of the dripping pickle she had brought upstairs with her. She offered me a bite and I chomped down, wiping pickle juice from my chin as I thought about overwhelming masculinity. That's what Jordan had. Maybe that was what gave him his aura of power. "Go on," I said.

"She had no choice. He was taking the
kiss from her. Stealing it, just as he
had stolen all those precious gems. She
closed her eyes as he bent his head
toward her, claiming her lips. Florinda
tried to struggle, but then everything
faded except the pressure of his body
against hers and the intensity of his
demanding mouth.

"Wow," Dannalee said. "Can you imagine somebody claiming your lips?"

I closed my eyes and saw Jordan's head bending toward

me, his laser eyes probing my very soul, his mouth ready to claim mine.

Dannalee poked me. "Was it like that when R. G. kissed you? I mean, did everything else fade except the intensity of his demanding mouth?"

I turned off Jordan and thought back about R. G.'s kiss. He had just sort of laid his lips on mine. It had been as exciting as kissing my own hand.

"Not exactly," I told Dannalee.

"Hey," she said, "I just had an idea. Why don't you run on a romance platform? Promise noontime seminars on kissing. Set up a junior-class dating bureau. Plan the most romantic prom this side of Lawrence Welk."

"Dannalee. . . ."

Dannalee waved her pickle in the air. "Pink campaign posters. We'll set up a 'Dial-Some-Heavy-Breathing' number."

"Dannalee. . . ."

She giggled. "You don't buy?"

"Who would conduct the kissing seminars—you and me?"

"Maybe we could get some experience before then. The least you can do, Trish, is have a little romance with Jordan. We could do an article in the school paper about candidates falling in love while they were running against one another."

"Dannalee. . . ."

"Jordan's awful sexy," she said. "It might be fun."

"*Dannalee!* Cut it out!"

"Okay, okay." She got up and started gathering up poster boards and paints. "I guess we'd better get over to R. G.'s. He'll have some good ideas about what we should do."

"Rescued by the poor student who turns out to be a rich farmer," I said.

Dannalee grinned. "See? Romance wherever you turn."

Something was bothering me. "Dannalee, have you ever noticed that in all the romances your mom writes, some guy is always coming along to rescue the girl when she gets into a jam? She never gets herself out of it herself."

Dannalee shrugged. "Sounds good to me. Especially if he's handsome and rich and can make things fade away with the intensity of his kisses."

"Oh, Dannalee, be serious. Isn't that what those romances say? That the solution to a girl's problems is to get a man to take care of her and make her happy?"

"Don't you want to get married?" Dannalee asked. "Don't you want a husband and kids?"

"Sure, I do. But does that mean I'm not allowed to do my own thing?"

"Maybe that *is* your own thing."

"But what if it isn't?"

"What does this have to do with running for junior-class president?" Dannalee asked.

I sighed. "Nothing, I guess. Maybe I just O.D.ed on romance. Forget what I said."

"I will," Dannalee said cheerfully. She handed me a box of drawing pencils to carry. "Do you know who I'd like to have claim my lips, Trish?"

I ran our male acquaintances through my mental computer. Jordan was the obvious one. Dannalee couldn't be in love with Jordan, too, could she?

"I can't guess," I said. I didn't want to hear if it was Jordan.

73

Dannalee giggled. "R. G.," she said. "I'd like to have R. G. kiss me. He has the nicest mouth of any guy I know."

R. G.! I slumped in relief. R. G.? I wondered how long Dannalee had had the hots for him. R. G.—but he was *my* friend. *My* neighbor.

Suddenly I was annoyed at Dannalee. "Let's go do some work," I said. "Don't you ever think about anything but romance, Dannalee?"

I didn't have my bike, and we had to carry the art stuff anyway, so we walked the mile to R. G.'s. We found him roosting on the roof of his pigpen playing his tuba. His hog run looked really nice. He had been working on it for a long time and had fenced off a rocky corner of his dad's pasture that had a little stream running through it. There were a couple of chokecherry trees in there among the rocks. R. G. had dug a kind of trench off to the side of the stream to create a nice muddy wallow. A couple of his pigs were lying in there now, grunting softly to themselves as they listened to his tuba serenade. Some others were rooting around in the shade of the chokecherry tree.

"This is the nicest hog run I've ever seen, R. G.," I said when he had finished his concert.

R. G. climbed down from the pigpen and surveyed his pigs. "They're my college money," he said. "They'll bring home the bacon—no, they'll *be* the bacon—so I can go to school. I figure the least I can do is let them enjoy their pig-hood while they can. I have to sell one of them pretty soon to pay for Belch's repairs."

His eyes were a little sad as he looked at his pigs. I had never seen him like that before. I had lived next to him all my life, and here all of a sudden was an R. G. I didn't know.

"Do you play music for them every day?" Dannalee asked.

R. G. grinned. "Not every day. But I need the practice, and they're a nice, uncritical audience." He tucked his tuba under his arm, and we headed toward the house. "I've got to start supper. We can work on those posters for a while, then we'll eat while I tell you about this idea I got while I was playing for my pigs."

Dannalee trotted alongside R. G., chattering up at him . . . probably wishing he'd bend his head and claim her lips.

I wondered what the two of them had done the day R. G. went to Dannalee's house to get the bra for his Tootsie costume. Had they talked about the coming campaign? Or had they whispered secret things that didn't include me?

What did I care?

I yanked my thoughts around and beamed them toward Jordan. But they kept straying back to the day R. G. had taken his shirt off in my room and I had wanted to be pulled close to his rock-hard chest.

8

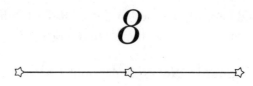

R. G. WAS ALL WIRED UP ABOUT HIS IDEA. He told Dannalee and me to sit down and take notes while he made supper for the three of us and told us his idea.

"What are we having?" Dannalee asked.

I never could figure out how she could stay so skinny when she was so interested in food all the time. Maybe that was one of the reasons why she was attracted to R. G. He was always putting together wonderful things to eat.

"It's a secret supper," R. G. said. He started breaking eggs into a bowl. "Now for my idea." Pulling an eggbeater from a drawer, he applied it to the eggs. "Susu is doing a hatchet job on your character, right, Trish?" His voice jiggled a little as he spun the wheel of the eggbeater.

"Right," Dannalee and I echoed. Dannalee jiggled her voice in imitation of R. G.'s, and he grinned at her before he went on. I tried to read things into that grin. I mean, I was really a little bent out of shape by Dannalee's wishing she could practice kissing him. I wondered if something big had been going on between them that I had been too dumb to notice.

Dannalee gave him back one of her Dannalee Specials, a twinkly kind of a smile that tucked dimples into her cheeks. I tried to look at Dannalee the way a guy might see her. Today she was wearing a high-necked white blouse with puffed sleeves and a kind of ratty, longish, blue-flowered skirt. On her feet were some knee-high, lace-up brown boots that had belonged to her grandmother and that Dannalee loved to wear. On anybody else, her clothes would have looked like ragbag rejects, but on Dannalee they had a sort of flair. Or I guess it was Dannalee who had the flair. Kind of like Audrey Hepburn in the movie *My Fair Lady*.

I couldn't deny that she was a real cute girl. If she wanted to practice kissing with R. G., I didn't think she would have much trouble getting the message across.

But why should I care? It was Jordan I was interested in.

Wasn't it?

Sometimes I wish the three of us could have stayed at age ten all our lives. At that age R. G. and Dannalee and I played together just as *kids*, without worrying about all the guy-and-girl stuff. Things were so simple then. We used to play a game called "Indian Maiden" a lot. R. G. was Big Chief Thunderbolt and he was always rescuing Divine Moon (Dannalee) and Murmuring Water (me) from one disaster after another.

Funny, I thought. *Even then we figured our destiny was in the hands of some guy, just like in Mrs. Davis' romantic stories.*

"Hey, Trish," R. G. said. He cupped his hands around his mouth. "Calling Trish Harker. Are you there, Trish?"

I had been lost inside my own head too long.

"Present," I said. "Speak."

R. G. flicked a thumb at me, exchanging another grin with Dannalee. "She's probably having a vision of herself in the White House or something." Turning to me, he said, "What I asked, Madam President, is what you think of my idea."

"Sorry," I said. "Guess I was off in the clouds somewhere. Run it by me again, will you?"

"What I'm suggesting," R. G. said, "is that we use what Susu has been doing to our own advantage. We'll make some 'Harker and her Barker' signs of our own."

Dannalee was already sketching a dog face. "Like, we can use the same setup that she did, only we'll put our own words on it. Maybe 'Harker and her Barker—Defenders of the Junior-Class Honor.' Something like that."

"I like it," I said. "We could tie it in with the treasure chest idea we talked about before. We could have one poster that says something like 'What secret campaign promise are Harker and her Barker guarding?'"

"Hey, that's good," R. G. said. "We can build up suspense until the election assembly the day before we vote." He poured what he had been mixing into a soufflé dish and stuck it into the oven.

"Everybody loves secrets." I pointed to the secret supper.

"I'll tell you mine if you'll tell me yours," R. G. said. "What *is* your secret campaign promise?"

I sighed. "It's such a secret that even *I* don't know yet."

"We'll think of something." R. G. began chopping up

things for a salad. "The main thing is to get the mystery going."

"I'll have the posters ready by Wednesday," Dannalee said. She already had both Snyde's and my faces drawn. It was interesting to see what she had done. Susu's drawings had been caricatures of our faces. Dannalee's sketch was a caricature of Susu's caricature. Instead of mean and threatening, our expressions now were kind of secretive, as if we knew something that nobody else knew . . . like the expression on the Mona Lisa's face.

"That's really good," I told Dannalee. "Nobody could take Susu's dagger work seriously after they see this."

I pictured Jordan looking at the posters.

"Very amusing," he would say in a suave voice. "Trish is running a very sophisticated campaign."

I liked those words. Suave Jordan. Sophisticated Trish. What a pair we could be. My fantasy shifted focus to a newspaper headline: "Suave Governor Jordan Avery and His Sophisticated Wife, Trish, Attend Inauguration Ball."

But first I had to make him see me as someone creative and imaginative, someone smooth and sophisticated.

I had a long way to go.

"R. G.," I said, "what kind of platform do you think Jordan will be running on? I mean, what kind of campaign promises is *he* going to make?"

R. G. put his salad on the table, which he had spread with a blue cloth. "I don't know if he'll promise anything. I think Jordan is going to run a razzle-dazzle, popularity-contest type of campaign. I doubt if he's even thought about what he wants to do if he does become junior-class president." R. G. took his mother's best blue and white dishes from a cupboard and dealt them around the table. "The thing about Jordan," he continued, "is that he's crazy for power, but I'm not sure he knows what he wants to do with it if he gets it."

"Power?" I had never really analyzed what Jordan was after in his energetic pushes to get somewhere.

"Power," R. G. repeated. "Jordan wants to be able to tell people what to do."

R. G. made Jordan sound like Hitler. It made me a little mad at R. G. What did he know about Jordan? I got even more peeved at R. G. when he asked Dannalee to help him arrange everything on the table and told *me* to go out to cut a few blue delphinium spikes for a centerpiece. I wondered what he wanted to say to Dannalee while I was gone.

I was a little happier when we got around to eating. R. G.'s supper was a wonder. Besides his secret soufflé, we had the salad, bran muffins, and frozen lemon pudding.

Dannalee sighed as we finished the dessert. "What I can't figure out is how a *guy* can do a meal like this. Roger Gregory Cole, you're terrific." Leaning her chin on her hands, she gazed at him with what could have been phony admiration, but could have been real.

R. G., the big ox, blushed and stammered. I almost expected him to scuff his foot and say, "Aw, shucks, ma'am, twarn't nuthin'."

But what he said was, "Thanks, Dannalee. You're all right yourself."

When I got home, Snyde and I walked to the upper pasture to bring the cows home for milking. Fetching the cows was the high spot of Snyde's day. It was his moment of power.

He was in charge. If any of the cows wandered off the long, winding lane into the surrounding fields, Snyde nipped their heels and barked them back into line with an enormous display of authority.

Was that what Jordan wanted? To herd people around? But surely it would be for some good purpose, something that would make their lives better. And I wanted to be by his side, be his Chief Enabler, as Mrs. Devane called it in our psychology class, devoting myself to him, doing what I could to help him make the most of himself.

Something niggled at my mind when I thought of spending my life promoting Jordan. Who would *I* be? What would become of the me inside of me who had had a moment or two of wondering what it would be like to *win* the election?

But wouldn't it be enough just to be part of Jordan?

A yip from Snyde broke into my thoughts. He was scuttling toward me, a cow in hot pursuit. The cow's head was lowered, and she was glaring at him, challenging him. Snyde was offended and protesting.

Was that my answer? Would Jordan be offended if my campaign began to look *too* good?

On the other hand, he wouldn't be interested in a wispy nothing he could beat without any effort at all.

Across the road, Mrs. Toomey was going out to put her chickens to bed. "We're marching on to glory," she sang. "We're working for our crown."

The murmur of the creek and the soft rasping of the crickets provided an orchestral accompaniment to Mrs. Toomey's quavering voice. A new moon was escaping from the peaks of Angel's Roost.

If only Jordan were there right at that moment, bending his dark head and claiming my lips, I could forget all of my unsettling thoughts.

Sighing, I headed toward the barn to milk the cows.

I knew something was going to go wrong the next day. Some days you just have those vibes. I was tired because I had stayed up late to do my homework, and then had got up early again to help Dad with the morning chores. But I took special pains with my appearance, anyway. This was the day all candidates for school offices would be introduced at noon on the quad. I had to pay attention to my image.

I used my curling iron to make my hair look soft around my face. Then I wasn't sure that was the image I wanted to project, so I wet my hair and let it hang straight, as usual.

I wore my dusty blue dress because Dannalee's *Dress the Part* book says that blue is a sincere color.

I guess Jordan read the *Dress the Part* book, too, because at noon on the quad I saw that he was also wearing blue. Sky blue shirt and navy blue pants. His eyes were kind of in between the two colors, so he was like a symphony in blue.

My knees got weak when I saw him. He was looking great that day. His curly hair stood at crisp attention. His eyes lasered the campus, noticing everybody, and making everybody notice him. His lips drew back over those forceful teeth of his, and he spread his smile around as if he had just created the world and was inviting everybody to enjoy it. Even the zits which sometimes plague his face had taken the day off, and his skin looked smooth and fresh. It was as if heaven were smiling down on its favorite son, and of course with that much approval aimed at him, there wasn't much left to spill over on me.

Susu was there looking as if she had created him.

Looking at the two of them, I just knew I was going to find manure on my shoes or a button would pop off my dress just as I went up on that platform to be introduced.

Even Dannalee noticed Jordan's perfection that day.

"He must have taken a charm pill this morning," she said. "But don't let that intimidate you, Trish."

All I really cared about was looking good enough that he wouldn't be embarrassed at running against such a nerd.

I think the whole student body was out there on the quad for the introductions. Some of them sat on the grass, still eating lunch. Some tossed a football back and forth. Some lounged around as if this were the most boring thing yet to be dreamed up by the school administration.

Mr. Barmy, our principal, climbed up on the platform that had been set up in the middle of the quad and raised his arms for silence. He didn't get it, but he went on, anyway.

"We're here today," he hollered, "to introduce next year's school officers. They are here among the candidates, but we won't know which ones they are until the voting on Friday."

He started with those who were running for sophomore-class offices. Some just got up and waved to the crowd, and others threw out candy kisses. I wished that I had thought of something like that to do.

Mr. Barmy progressed through those running for junior-class offices. It was Jordan's turn.

Jordan buttered everybody up with a smile as he leaped to the platform, his vitality spilling all over the crowd. And he didn't say a single thing because his carefully rehearsed friends said it all. They chanted:

"Every Pratt High resident
Wants Avery for president."

Jordan strutted around the platform with his arms held out in a wide V as they chanted. Then, just before it began to get tiresome, he jumped back off the platform.

How could I follow that?

I didn't stumble as I climbed the stairs to the platform. That gave me a little confidence. There were a few scattered cheers, probably from my Wolf Creek classmates.

"I have a big secret," I said into the mike that had been set up for the introductions. My voice blared back at me from the speakers, but I was used to giving speeches, so that didn't bother me.

"How big is your secret?" somebody yelled back.

"So big that it takes a chest to carry it in. There will be clues around the campus next week about what's in my treasure chest."

I looked out over the audience and saw R. G. and Dannalee standing together. R. G.'s head was bent toward her, and he was smiling down at her. She was giving him her Dannalee Special.

It threw me.

"Uh, look for it," I said. "Then come to the election assembly on Thursday, and I'll show you my chest."

Before the words were out of my mouth I knew they were all wrong. Flustered, I tried to smile, and then decided the best thing to do was escape, while everybody was laughing.

But I slipped going down the steps and pitched onto the grass, landing right next to somebody's bologna sandwich. Everybody laughed harder, as if this was part of the show. I might have been able to pull it off if I hadn't heard Susu singsonging that age-old rhyme we tormented each other with in grade school:

"I see London, I see France, I see Trish's underpants."

I had attracted Jordan's attention, all right. He was there putting out a hand to help me up. Riley was there, too. Before I could pull my skirt down, his camera clicked, and another disaster was recorded for posterity.

9

I'VE NEVER BEEN CAUGHT IN QUICKSAND, but I know what it must feel like. I've heard that the more you struggle, the more you sink into the muck. That's how I felt after I fell off the platform during the candidate introductions. No matter how I tried to make my campaign look good after that, I would just make things worse. Who was ever going to forget my dumb statement about showing my chest? And who was going to take me seriously after seeing me sprawled there with my skirts around my neck and Susu chanting that stupid rhyme?

I was sure Susu had plans for the picture Riley had snapped of me. And worst of all, how could I ever hope to make Jordan see me as sophisticated and creative after that?

I didn't even want to face the Wolf Creek kids on the school bus, so I was glad when R. G. asked Dannalee and me if we wanted to ride home with him in Belch. He said

Mr. McCabe at the auto shop wanted to get rid of it before it ruined his reputation.

I had a lot of sympathy for that poor old car. I felt we were both rolling disasters.

Dannalee decided to take the bus home. "I promised Dad I'd ride up around Angel's Roost and look for some lost cattle right after school, and you know the way Belch is. We might not get home until next week." She gave us a smile as she headed toward the school bus. "I know I can trust the two of you alone."

Just a gentle reminder to me that I shouldn't try to make time with her guy. Why is it that when a girl falls in love, she thinks every other girl in town is after her love interest? Dannalee knew I had never been interested in R. G. other than as a friend. *I* wasn't the one who thought he had the most kissable lips of any guy at Pratt High. I looked at R. G.'s lips now as we started walking toward Belch. I remembered the night he had kissed me. I had thought if that was all there was to kissing, I could do without it. But I hadn't been prepared for that kiss. It might be nice to try it again. R. G. did have a nice mouth. Not as interesting as Jordan's, but still, it was wide and generous, and his lips were sort of soft-looking.

But what was I doing thinking about kissing R. G. when Dannalee had just warned me to keep my hands off him? What kind of a friend was I, anyway?

Belch backfired a couple of times as we drove through Pratt after picking up some groceries R. G. needed. We thought Traxler might come after us, accusing us of torpedoing the place, but he must have been somewhere arresting a little old lady whose dog do-doed on somebody's lawn. We didn't see him.

"R. G.," I said when we got on the highway and Belch was sputtering its way up Indian Ridge, "R. G., don't you think I should just quit this dumb campaign? I mean, I've already lost. I ought to spend the next two weeks studying for finals, not giving CPR to a dead cause."

"Dead!" R. G. said. "It's a long way from dead. Look, what's going to be the main topic of conversation around campus for the next few days?" Without waiting for me to answer, he went on. "Your chest, that's what." We both flushed. "Oh, you know. Your *treasure* chest."

"Yeah." Black shrouds hung around the word.

"Well, that's the first thing we'll display on Monday morning. Here's what we can do. You know how Jordan's going to start the campaign with the band and all?"

"Pretty fancy opener," I muttered.

"Yours can be just as good." R. G. paused while he nursed Belch, backfiring and clanking, over the crest of Indian Ridge. "What we'll do is put Belch's top down and rig a shelf up on the back of the seat there. We'll have to find some kind of old trunk and have a sign saying something like 'Herein lies Trish's secret campaign promise.' You'll sit on the top of the backseat, waving like the Queen of England. The kids will love it."

"They'll laugh."

"Let 'em. They'll see what a good sport you are and that you can turn a disaster into a triumph."

I thought about it. I would look good if I came out of this thing smiling. It would impress Jordan if I rose like a phoenix from such a complete wipeout.

"I'll do it," I told R. G.

"Atta girl," he said.

I called Dannalee on Saturday morning to tell her that R. G. and I were going to locate an old trunk or something for my treasure chest. She was enthusiastic.

"Let's make a banner that says 'Trish for President,' and you can drape it across your chest."

"That's great," I said. "R. G. and I may even paint it with the school colors, too."

There was a second's silence, and then Dannalee said, "You're going to paint your *chest?*"

"The *treasure* chest, silly. The one we'll be trucking around on the back of R. G.'s car."

"Well, I'm talking about *your* chest, to put the banner across. Like Miss America. It *would* be kind of interesting, though, if you painted it in the school colors."

"Cut it out, Dannalee. We're going to conduct this campaign with *dignity.*"

"We can try," Dannalee said. "But I'm betting this campaign will be one Pratt High will never forget."

After I finished talking with Dannalee, I went over to see Mrs. Toomey. She had some old trunks, and I hoped she would lend us one to be my treasure chest.

Climbing the stone steps to her skinny, weather-beaten house, I stopped to listen. I wanted to check out her mood for the day.

"There is sunshine in my soul today," she was warbling, "and hope and praise and love. . ."

I went up the rest of the steps and knocked on the door.

". . . for blessings which He gives me now," Mrs. Toomey sang as she came to the door, "and joys laid up above."

"Well, my stars," she said, opening the door and peering out at me, "if it isn't Gloria. Come on in and sit a spell."

The years have gone by too fast for Mrs. Toomey. She never can quite keep up with how fast Gloria and Marv and I have grown.

"How are you, Mrs. Toomey?" I went inside while she held the screen door, shooing back a couple of pesky flies. It shut with the creak of ancient hinges when she let go of it.

"Oh, the good Lord's given me another fine day," Mrs. Toomey said. She hurried over to the golden oak cupboard that stood in one corner of her kitchen, her joints creaking almost as loud as the screen-door hinges. Opening one of the cupboard doors, she pulled out a large, battered tin container.

"Just baked these today." She held the container toward me.

I knew it held ginger cookies. Ever since my childhood I had fished ginger cookies out of that container. Mrs. Toomey's kitchen always smelled comfortably of baking bread or cookies, spicy aromas of cinnamon and nutmeg seeping into every corner. It was the kind of place where you felt at home even if you'd never been there before. I had always thought I'd want a kitchen just like that someday.

"Don't have anybody around to eat these anymore," Mrs. Toomey said, "but I can't seem to get out of the habit."

Mrs. Toomey's husband was dead and her seven children were scattered all over the country. I knew the church ladies stopped by frequently, and R. G. went over there every few days to see what he could do to help her. Mom checked with her every day, but I felt ashamed that I hadn't been there more often. Not only to eat her cookies, but also just to visit.

"It's nice to see you, Gloria," she said as I munched a cookie. Then she tipped her head back to look at me through her bifocals. "Why, it's not Gloria at all. It's little Trish. Why didn't you tell me? I'm getting so foolish these days, I hardly know my own self. Not that it's any great pleasure to know that old woman who looks out of my mirror." Chuckling, she offered me another cookie.

"Mrs. Toomey." I swallowed the last bite of my first cookie and took another one. "I was just wondering if I could borrow one of your old trunks. You know, the ones that belonged to your mother and you used to let me play with?"

"Sure, honey." Mrs. Toomey motioned for me to sit down at her big round oak table. "Tell me why you want to borrow one of those old things so I'll know the right one to give you."

While I told her, my eyes wandered around her cozy kitchen. I remembered the Siamese cat salt and pepper shakers in the center of the table from the days when I came visiting with Mom. Mrs. Toomey had bought them in San Francisco when she had visited her oldest daughter there right after World War II, when the girl had been a WAVE. She had bought the pink china girl who held toothpicks in her wide skirt in Seattle, when her second child, a son, was married there in 1952. Mrs. Toomey is proud of all of her children and loves to tell about them.

"Well, now, that's right nice," she said when I finished telling about the coming election and my part in it. "I'd be right proud to have you use a trunk of mine. It's to be a treasure chest, you say?"

"That's what we'll be calling it." My eyes skipped across the faces of her children, whose pictures were displayed on an old oak buffet standing near the table. Seven of them. "Our best crop," she always said of them. "Mine and Orlando's."

Mrs. Toomey stood up. "I know just the one you ought to use." Beckoning for me to follow, she headed for a back bedroom.

In a dark closet, she unearthed a wooden chest covered by a faded bedspread. It was about two feet long and maybe a foot high and fifteen inches wide. It was decorated with broad bands of tarnished metal, and there was an enormous metal lock on its front. Perfect for a treasure chest, although of course we wouldn't be painting *that* in our school colors.

"If you'd just lift it out, dear, we'll empty it, and you can take it with you." Mrs. Toomey twitched the old bedspread that had covered it, releasing a cloud of ancient dust.

The chest was not large, but it was heavy. I heaved it out of the closet and onto a chair. Mrs. Toomey fussed at the lock, and I thought for a minute we might have to use a different chest if she couldn't get it open. Already I wanted that particular chest; it was just the kind to hold a secret.

I just wished I knew the secret—my secret campaign promise. Sometime soon I would have to decide what it was going to be.

There was a snap as the lock opened. "There it is," Mrs. Toomey said. "It's been a long time since I opened it. Couldn't remember just how to do it."

She lifted the lid of the chest, and I saw it was filled with music. Sheets of music. Books of music. Handwritten pages of music. I saw that one of the books was entitled *Advanced Studies for the Violin.*

"I didn't know anybody in your family played the violin," I said.

"Oh, pshaw, it's been so long ago I'd almost forgotten myself," she said.

I picked up one of the sheets of music. The name "Christina Larsen Toomey" was written across it.

"It was you, wasn't it?" I asked. "*You* used to play the violin."

"Yes," she said. "Yes. I did." Digging down into the chest, she brought up a stack of music and slowly sorted through it. "I've forgotten all these pieces. Funny how they all seemed so important to me once," she said softly.

I looked at the complex music. "You must have been very good. Why did you stop playing?"

Mrs. Toomey fingered the music. "Oh, lands, who had time for violin sawing when there was tomatoes to can and haying crews to cook for and kids to tend to?"

"But it was something you loved," I insisted. "Wasn't it?"

"Oh, my, yes. Never thought I could give it up. But Orlando . . . well, he said I could play after I got the garden watered and the mending done and the house taken care of and all." She shook her head. "Never could seem to get caught up. So I put all this stuff away. Thought I'd get it out when I had time." She was taking all of the music out of the chest and stacking it on a little table.

"So now you have time. You could play again now, couldn't you?"

Mrs. Toomey shook her head again, holding up her twisted hands. "It was important only to *me*, anyway. Just a woman's fancy. Nobody needed it." She sighed. "They needed the baking worse."

Maybe they did. I hadn't lived her life. How could I say her music might have been just as important? I knew that her children always praised her baking when they came to see her. And they had turned out well, most of them college graduates. One a doctor. Another a professor. A daughter who was in state politics. Her best crop.

But all that music. I wondered if I could give up something I loved that much for Jordan. Of course I could, I decided. Just let him ask.

I carried the chest into the kitchen, where Mrs. Toomey wrapped a stack of her cookies in wax paper and put them inside it. "Take them to Marv," she said. "He always liked this kind."

"Marv is away at college," I told her. "He probably won't be home for another week or so."

"Pshaw, I keep forgetting. Seems like everybody grows up so fast and goes away." She put the lid back on the old tin container. "Maybe I should stop baking so much."

I hoped she wouldn't. It would be too much to put that aside along with her dusty music.

As I went back down the stone steps, I heard her singing again. "Come, come ye saints, no toil nor labor fear, but with joy wend your way. . ."

I was really pleased with the chest. As I walked across the road and down our willow-shaded lane, I thought how nice it would look on the back of Belch on Monday morning. I was really getting kind of excited about the whole thing.

For a moment I thought the car parked in our yard was Belch, and I wondered why R. G. would drive over when it was just as easy to run across the fields. But then I saw it wasn't Belch at all. In the first place, it wasn't a convertible. In the second place, it was a much later model. Then I realized whose car it was. Jordan's.

Jordan's car was sitting in our driveway.

10

IN MY SOCIAL SCIENCE CLASS, Mr. Roper has been talking about deductive reasoning. That's where you draw a conclusion from a set of premises. Like, a car doesn't go from one place to another without a driver; Jordan's car was there; therefore Jordan must be nearby.

I couldn't believe it. That's like coming home to find the president of the United States visiting. Something you don't even think about because it just isn't going to happen.

What could Jordan be doing at my house? And where was he? Could he have gone inside already? Oh, not through the back porch, the way we all did. Not past the baskets of eggs waiting to be cleaned and the manure-covered boots we wore out to the barn. Not past the shelf where Mom stored stacks of toilet paper and cans of Drano and Snyde's flea powder.

Oh, God, I prayed, *let him have gone in through the front door.*

I thought of our living room. The sagging green couch.

Dad's newspapers scattered all over the floor in front of the TV. Jordan's family wouldn't have a TV in the living room. People with class have a separate TV room.

What else, what else? The wash, that's what else. Mom likes to dry the wash outside in good weather, and just before I went over to Mrs. Toomey's I had brought it all in from the clotheslines and had dumped it on the sagging green sofa. In front of the tacky TV set. With messy newspapers scattered all around.

Oh, God, I prayed, *forget what I said. Let Jordan still be outside.*

I thought about going back to Mrs. Toomey's until he left. But Mom saw me through the kitchen window and called to me. "Trish, there's a friend of yours here to see you."

Not in the kitchen. Thinking about it, I groaned. The smells of cooking. Not cookies like in Mrs. Toomey's kitchen, but probably cabbage or maybe miscellaneous chicken parts for Snyde. Mom's genealogy books spread all over the table. The Anderson Lumber Company calendar hanging on the wall. The cartoons attached to the refrigerator door with little magnets shaped like cucumbers and onions. And Snyde doing something gross like smelling Jordan's pants leg.

Mom was making bread and was up to her elbows in whole-wheat flour and yeast and wheat germ and all that stuff she puts into the bread to make it nutritious. She was explaining to Jordan, just the way she does to R. G., the benefits of whole-wheat flour (you get bran that helps prevent problems in your digestive tract—can a body actually die from embarrassment?). Jordan was nodding and asking questions about how the yeast works and if a loaf of bread can "fall" the way a cake does.

97

He grinned as I came into the kitchen, still clutching Mrs. Toomey's little wooden chest, which I hurriedly stashed on a chair, which I then pushed as close as possible to the table. I didn't want him asking questions.

A quick glance around told me that at least Snyde wasn't in there being obnoxious.

"I'm getting an education," Jordan said. "It's fascinating."

"Bread?" I said. Bread was fascinating? Bread was bread. Mom made a batch every week.

"Trish makes good bread, too," Mom told Jordan. "Her specialty is banana nut."

If I really did die from embarrassment, could they put Mom on trial for murder?

"Jordan doesn't care about bread, Mom," I choked.

"Yes, I do, Trish." Jordan turned his face toward me. I had never been that close to him before. I wanted to reach out and touch the mole on his cheek with my finger. The afternoon light coming through the dangling crystals Mom had hung in one window made colored patches on his face and hair, like a hundred miniature spotlights with colored gels.

"My mother thinks bread grows in plastic bags," Jordan said. "She's not big on baking. I've never seen anyone make bread before."

Jordan's mother. Emily Avery, attorney-at-law. How could I have ever thought I wanted to be like her? No, I would be homemaker-wife, mixing batches of fascinating bread for Jordan every week.

"Some women are good at apple pies and tarts," Mom said, "and others are better at affidavits and torts."

Jordan laughed. "That's very good, Mrs. Harker."

Mom smiled modestly.

"I wasn't putting my mother down," Jordan went on. "She's one of the most interesting people I've ever known. You can always depend on her to keep a conversation lively."

In my mental library, I pulled out the newly installed cookbooks and put back the discarded law books.

I wondered what I could say that would show Jordan that I, too, was a brilliant conversationalist.

"Uh. . ." I said. I strained to think. My brain was melting Jell-O. My tongue was a Popsicle stick rattling against the picket fence of my teeth.

Mom saved the day. Wiping flour from her arms onto a kitchen towel, she said, "I know you young folks have things to talk about. Let me make sure there's a place to sit in the living room."

We followed her as she swooped through the mess in the living room, gathering up the wash and the newspapers in one smooth action. I wondered where mothers learn little bits of magic like that. The room was presentable now, even though the green couch still sagged. But at least I wouldn't have to introduce Jordan to mounds of my clean underwear.

"Won't you sit down?" I said, surprised at how gracious I sounded. I was getting my cool back.

Jordan sat. "I was just driving through Wolf Creek and thought I'd stop and wish you well in the campaign next week."

Suave Jordan. *Kind* Jordan. He wanted me to know he wasn't going to use the embarrassing things that had happened to me the day before against me.

"I wish you well, too," I said.

"We can't let a little thing like running for the same office ruin our friendship, can we, Trish?"

What friendship? I didn't even know we'd had one. But maybe—just maybe—Jordan had been secretly in love with me for a long time the way I had been with him. Maybe *he* had been waiting for a chance to make *me* notice *him*. This was like a dream come true.

Then I heard something I didn't want to hear. The *pah! pah! pah!* of a tuba. Deductive reasoning told me that to make a sound like that a tuba must be blown; since the tuba was making those sounds, somebody was blowing it.

That somebody had to be R. G.

And from the direction of the sounds, he was rapidly approaching our back door.

I couldn't have R. G. barging in right then. Maybe Jordan hadn't heard the sounds. Maybe Mom would say I was busy and would send R. G. away.

But Jordan *had* heard. "What's that?" He looked puzzled.

"Oh," I said, thinking desperately, "we've got this funny telephone." I giggled loudly. "You know how some people have telephones that tinkle." I was getting into trouble. "Wait here. I'll go answer it." I hurried to the kitchen.

"R. G.'s coming," Mom said. She was elbow deep in flour still. "Shall I keep him here in the kitchen?"

Mom understood, bless her.

"No," I whispered. "He'd probably hear Jordan and me talking. You'd better send him up to my room. Tell him I'll be up in a minute."

I whisked back to the living room, pulling the door closed behind me. "Just had to take care of some business."

"Hope it wasn't election business." Jordan gave me one of his smiles, the kind that makes you forget that he's not all that good-looking and not very tall and that his ears are big and he sometimes has zits. "Are you as excited about this whole thing as I am, Trish? I mean about the election? It's going to be fun, don't you think?" His voice had changed from suave to boyish. There were so many Jordans. I didn't know which one I liked best. I liked them all! I *loved* them all!

"I'm excited, too." I could hear footsteps going up the stairs, but at least R. G. wasn't *oompah*ing his tuba any more.

Snyde must have come in with R. G. because he nosed through the door, which I evidently hadn't shut all the way, and ambled into the living room. Sitting down abruptly, he scratched a flea, his leg thumping against the floor. That didn't do enough, so he twisted around to bite at himself, making loud snapping noises with his teeth.

Jordan stared at him thoughtfully.

I was sure that Emily Avery, attorney-at-law, would never allow a dog inside her house. I wondered how I could boot Snyde out without making Jordan think I was cruel to animals.

"Isn't that the dog that your brother used to put a wig on and call his Aunt Beulah?" Jordan asked.

"He was just being silly," I stammered. "Oh, Jordan, I heard you're going to stage a real spectacular on Monday to open your campaign." I hadn't meant to bring that up, but I had to say something.

He turned his attention back to me. "Did that leak out? I hoped to keep it as a surprise." He laughed a little. "Sometimes I think there's a spy behind every tree."

I wondered if he thought *I* had been spying behind trees.

"Somebody just mentioned that you were going to have a band and parade and all that," I ran on. "They just merely mentioned it."

"Is that all they mentioned? Just the band and parade?"

I tried to remember if there was anything else that Dannalee had told me that Blair Bates had told her that Sheila Moss had told him that Glen Daley had told her that Amelia Slade had told him that Jordan had said. What more *could* he be going to do?

"I think so," I said.

"No problem, then." Jordan sounded relieved. "I imagine you have something really big planned, too, don't you, Trish?"

Suddenly my plans didn't seem so big at all, especially if he was going to do *more* than the band and parade. I was going to look like a total idiot perched on the back of Belch with Mrs. Toomey's little wooden chest if Jordan was going to have the entire United States Air Force flying overhead or something.

"Oh, I'm not really doing much," I said.

Jordan was looking at the ceiling, and I realized R. G. was playing his tuba up there in my room.

He smiled. "Your *telephone* again?"

I gave a shaky little whinny. Without trying to explain anything, I said, "I just don't have good ideas the way you do, Jordan. I wish I did, but I just can't think of them. They just don't occur to me." I was babbling to cover up those blats of R. G.'s tuba. How could I explain to Jordan what R. G. was doing in my bedroom playing the tuba?

Snyde stopped snapping at his fleas and sprawled out in the middle of the floor, licking at embarrassing parts of himself with juicy slurps.

"Oh, but you do have good ideas, Trish." Jordan's smile was beginning to look a little strained. "Your idea about displaying your treasure chest was a really good one."

I noticed he emphasized *treasure* so that I wouldn't be embarrassed again about what I had said at the introductions.

Wonderful, kind Jordan. He was trying to ignore all that was going on around us, too, trying to set me at ease.

"Thanks, Jordan. I'll do something with that idea."

The tuba sounds upstairs had stopped. I wondered why. Then I heard the creaking of the stairs, and I knew why. R. G. was coming down.

"Yes, that's a wonderful idea." I rattled on, not even knowing what I was saying. "Yes, I think I'll use the treasure chest idea." I tried to hear if R. G. was coming to the living room door. I wished Jordan would leave.

Jordan wasn't ready to leave. "I'll bet the secret campaign promise is something really good, isn't it, Trish? Some far-out class project or something like that, isn't it?"

If I had known what it was, I would have told him. "Could be, Jordan." I tried to look coy as I listened for R. G.'s footsteps. Mom was probably keeping him in the kitchen.

"Or some new idea for fund-raising?" Jordan suggested.

"That's a good idea." I watched Snyde roll over on his back, twitching back and forth as his four big paws dangled in the air and his tongue hung sideways out of his mouth. It was something he did a lot, but Jordan probably thought he was having a fit, because he stood up.

"I can see you're not going to tell me," he said with his big Jordan smile. "But listen, Trish, I'd really like to get together with you sometime. I know you're probably all dated up for tonight, but maybe some other time, after the election?"

This Jordan was hesitant, a little unsure of himself. I liked this one best of all.

"I'd like that, Jordan." I wished I dared say that I wasn't dated up that night at all, that I would leave with him that very instant if he wanted me to. But that would be dumb. If he thought my Saturday nights were a giddy whirl of fun, booked up weeks in advance, that was fine. Would a guy like Jordan want to date a girl whose biggest excitement on a Saturday night was deciding which cow to milk first?

"I'd like that, Jordan. I really would." He had no idea how *much* I'd like it.

I guided Jordan around Snyde, who stopped his twitching around and leaped to his feet to smell Jordan's trouser legs. Pushing him aside, I walked Jordan to the door.

"It's been nice talking to you, Trish." Reaching into a pocket, Jordan brought something out. Taking my hand, he said, "Here, I'd like to give you something."

It was a tiny, thumbprint-sized picture of him. Licking the back of it, he stuck it on my hand.

"Part of my campaign stuff," he said. "I'm giving you an advance preview." He turned to go.

I guess R. G. got away from Mom, because just then he opened the living room door and bumbled in.

"Hey, Trish, how long do you want me to wait for you in your bedroom?" he asked.

Jordan turned back, and the two guys stared at one another.

"Didn't know you had company," R. G. said. "Hi, Jordan."

"How ya doing?" Jordan said. "See you Monday, Trish." Walking quickly to his car, he got in and drove away.

Leaning weakly against the door frame, I watched him go.

11

"WHAT WAS JORDAN DOING HERE?" R. G. asked. "You been fraternizing with the enemy, Trish?"

"He just happened to be driving by," I said angrily. "Besides, this isn't exactly war, is it? I mean, I can *talk* with him, can't I? Just because we're running against one another doesn't mean we have to ruin our friendship, does it?" I hoped Jordan hadn't heard what R. G. said about waiting for me in my bedroom. What would he think of me? "Who asked *you* to come barging in like that, anyway?"

R. G. blinked. "I didn't know you were entertaining company, Trish. I came across the fields. I didn't see his car." His thoughts must have backpedaled a little because he said, "Since when have you and Jordan had this big friendship, anyway? I didn't know you knew him that well."

"There are a lot of things you don't know about me, R. G." I reached up to brush away some hair that had fallen in my eyes. Too late I realized that was the hand on which Jordan had pasted his picture.

R. G. reached out and took my hand, staring at the picture. Then he looked at me, his eyes full of questions.

"Oh, for gosh sakes, R. G.," I said. "We were just talking about our campaigns. He's going to use pictures like this for something, and he was just showing me. Is there anything wrong with that?" I pulled my hand away from R. G. and hid it behind my back. "What did you come over for?" I asked him.

R. G. still looked puzzled, but he said, "Strangely enough, I came for a picture of *you*."

"A picture? What are you going to do with it?"

"I'd rather not say until I find out if it will work. Any picture will do. A copy of your yearbook picture will be fine."

"I'm sure I have extras." I was curious about what he was going to do with the picture, but mainly I just wanted him to leave so I could replay the good parts of Jordan's visit. I could still hear his deep oboe voice saying, "I'd really like to get together with you sometime."

Walking over to the desk where Mom kept all her genealogy stuff, I stirred around in a box of pictures. "Here's one you can have." I handed R. G. a photo of me. "You're not going to do the same thing as Jordan did, are you?"

R. G. shook his head. "Nothing like that. It's just something Dannalee and I thought we'd try. If you need me, I'll be at her house."

"Fine." That thought didn't even bother me this time.

"Well." R. G. shifted his big feet. "I guess I'd better be going." Tucking my picture into his shirt pocket, he went back to the kitchen to pick up his tuba.

"I'll have hot bread in about an hour," Mom said, "if you want to stick around, R. G."

"That's a real temptation, Mrs. Harker. But I better go."

He went out, and we heard a mournful *oompaaaaah* as he started back across the fields.

"That's not like R. G. to refuse food." Mom's forehead creased in worry. "Did you two have a fight or something?"

"No, Mom, it's okay."

"I'm sorry I let him break in on you and Jordan. He came downstairs and asked where you were, and when I told him he went right in."

"It's all right, Mom."

"That other boy—Jordan. Is he the one you're running against?"

"Yes, Mom."

"Why in the world would he come to visit you just before election week?"

Mom was as bad as R. G. "We're just friends," I said. "It was just a friendly visit. I have to go do the dusting now, Mom."

As I went to start our weekly cleaning, I let my thoughts flow back to Jordan.

I thought about him all afternoon. I didn't think anything specific, like a wedding or anything. I just let the glory of him surround me like warm water, and I drifted on it, serene and content. I could explain away all the things that had happened while he was there, if he asked about them. The main thing was that he had come to see me.

I was still floating when Snyde and I went out to the barn that evening to help Dad with the chores. I joined right in with Mrs. Toomey who was singing, as usual, as she went to tend her chickens. "We are all enlisted 'til the conflict is o'er," we harmonized. "Happy are we! Happy are we!"

"We ought to go into show business," Mrs. Toomey called across the road. "We could call ourselves 'The Gospel Girls.'"

I laughed. "How about 'Hymns by the Hers?'" I called back.

Chuckling, she went into her henhouse, where I could hear her singing, "Soldiers in the army, there's a bright crown in store. We shall win and wear it by and by."

I went to the barn, listening to the crickets and night birds tuning up for their evening's performance. The spring moon hung over Angel's Roost, and a soft south wind whispered a duet with the creek.

The world had never been so beautiful.

"Well," Dad said as I wafted into the barn, "I guess we don't need electricity tonight. You could light up the whole place yourself."

"I'm happy, Dad."

He grinned. "Amazing what a fella can do to a girl. I saw him come to visit you. Him and his tuba."

Tuba! Dad thought I was all aglow over R. G. "Dad, it's not R. G. It's Jordan I like. The guy I'm running against."

"Oh?" Dad's eyebrows went up. "That's a little peculiar, isn't it? How come you're running against a fella you take such a shine to? I thought you liked R. G."

I couldn't explain it all to him. "I *do* like R. G., Dad, but as a friend. He's so—so ordinary."

"Never struck me that way." Dad picked up a milker and attached it to a cow, then came back to stand by me. "How's your campaign coming along, anyway?"

"It's going all right, Dad." I had already caught Jordan's attention. What more could I ask? "This next week will be kind of hard, but it will be fine."

"Look, Trish," Dad said, "if things get too much, you don't have to help me with the chores, you know. Don't try to be Superwoman and do everything at once."

"I can handle it, Dad."

He patted my shoulder awkwardly with his big, rough, farmer's hand. "Oh, I know how you feel you have to prove something to Marv. But you don't have to prove it to me, Trish. Sometimes you have to let some things go. If you decide you're too busy to help out here, it's okay with me."

"Thanks, Dad." I looked around the hay-fragrant barn. The spring calves blatted mournfully from their pen across the central aisle. The barn cats peered down from their home in the loft. The horses at the other end of the barn munched their oats and nickered softly in the twilight.

I loved this part of my life. It *was* hard to take care of all the work and do all that I needed to do at school, too. I would soon have to make a choice.

But I wasn't ready to give up helping Dad yet. He was right about my wanting to prove something to Marv. Maybe I had to prove something to myself, too. I wasn't quite sure what it was.

"Dad," I said, picking up a milker and heading for old Rosie, the Jersey cow, "how come Marv didn't come home this weekend?"

Dad shrugged. "He called and said he was busy. Marv's not all that interested in farm work, anyway. But that's his choice."

———

We found out the next day what it was Marv was busy with. He showed up with Susu beside him, right after church.

As they got out of Marv's little red Veedub, Snyde lumbered over to greet them, tail swishing and big jaws open in a friendly grin.

Susu climbed back into the car and slammed the door. Mom and I couldn't hear what she said from where we were watching through the kitchen window, but it must have been something strong. Marv seemed to do a little coaxing, but when Snyde jumped up and poked his snout through the open window, Susu squealed so loud we could hear her just fine.

Marv took Snyde by the collar and hauled him off toward our big elm tree, which was the anchor for a dog chain we kept for emergencies. He attached the chain to Snyde's collar, and then walked back to Susu, leaving Snyde straining to follow, his tail wagging wildly and his big face creased with bewilderment.

Marv ignored him. Susu stuck to Marv like a growth as they came into the house.

"Hi, Mom," Marv said. "Can you water down the soup?"

"There's plenty for everyone," Mom said. "Glad to have you. Pull up a couple more chairs. Dinner will be ready in about two minutes."

Marv introduced Susu to Mom and Dad. "I think you already know each other," he said when they turned to me.

"Oh, Trish and I have been friends since kindergarten," Susu said.

I wondered how she defined friends. "How are you, Susu?"

"Worn to a frazzle," she said. "I've been so-o-o-o-o busy on Jordan's campaign. Won't you be glad when it's all over and you can relax?"

I noticed she said "*you* can relax" as if it was just I who would be relaxing while she and Jordan and Company went on to get his administration set up.

"I'm relaxed now," I lied. "We got all of our preparations done early." I crossed my fingers behind my back the way we did when we were little kids and told a big fib.

"Jordan told me you're going ahead with your little treasure chest idea." Susu made it sound like something first graders would do. "I wish *our* problems were that simple."

So Jordan had reported to Susu after his trip to see me. If Susu was trying to upset me, she was doing a good job, but not for the reasons she thought. I wanted to end our little discussion, but first I thought I'd scare her a bit.

"Oh, our problems *aren't* that simple," I said. "Right now we're trying to find something big enough to haul all our equipment to Pratt tomorrow."

Susu looked uncertain. Her glance shot around the room, searching for clues as to what I was going to haul to Pratt.

Marv was getting uncomfortable. "I think it's time to eat," he said.

"Oh, we almost forgot the candy, Marv," Susu said. "Run out and get it."

Marv went out to the car as Susu went on. "I wanted you to know I don't hold any grudges about your dog coming after me last Saturday, Trish. So I'm contributing a little something to your campaign."

Marv came back with a big paper sack marked "Hanna's Sweet Shoppe." Susu took it from him and handed it to me.

"I don't know if you had thought of this already, but it's always a good idea to throw candy to the kids during election week. You can write 'Vote for Trish' on little stickers and put one on each piece of candy." Susu smiled as if she had just spilled the biggest campaign secret of the century.

Marv didn't look entirely happy about this whole thing. "You don't have to use it if you don't want to, Trish. Maybe you've already got everything planned."

The candy idea was nothing new, but still it was nice of Susu to buy it for me. It really surprised me.

"Thanks," I said. "That's nice of you, Susu."

"Dinner's getting cold," Mom announced.

It wasn't until after Marv and Susu left that I looked at the candy. Then I knew why Susu had given it to me. The bag was full of stale, rocklike chews that had been sitting in Hanna's Sweet Shoppe window for so long that they could be used as bullets. If I threw that kind of candy to the kids the next week, they'd throw it right back at me.

But the *idea* was good. It was too late to get good candy since I wanted it for first thing in the morning. I wondered what I could substitute. What would fit in with my treasure theme?

Pennies! R. G., Dannalee, and I had all been saving pennies for several years. We had started when we had been Chief Thunderbolt and the Indian Maidens and we had planned to buy a tepee. Saving pennies had become a habit.

I called up both R. G. and Dannalee. "Bring your penny pots," I said. "Emergency session at my house."

We spent the evening writing "Vote for Trish" on a whole lot of little yellow stickers that Mom used to flag things on her genealogy sheets. Then we wrapped each penny in aluminum foil and put a sticker on it.

I debated about telling them that I thought Jordan's and Susu's visits might be connected. Finally I decided I had to tell them at least some of what Jordan had said. After all, it had to have been Susu's idea in the first place. Jordan was just following the plans of his campaign manager.

"He really did a number on you," R. G. said when I finished telling all I was going to tell.

"What do you mean by that?" I demanded.

R. G. licked a yellow sticker and applied it to a wrapped penny. "Okay, I'll itemize." He held up one finger. "First. He threw you off balance by coming unexpectedly." R. G. held up another finger alongside the first. "Second. He let you know that it's all just fun and games, nothing to take seriously." Another finger sprang up. "Third. He let you know that his opening blast tomorrow will be even more spectacular than he let you find out already."

That was too much. "What do you mean, he *let* me find out? He didn't have anything to do with my finding out about his plans. You know as well as I do that it was Dannalee who told me that Blair told her that Sheila told him that Glen told her that Amelia told him."

"And *Jordan* told her," Dannalee finished. "I'll bet he *did* tell her purposely. You know what Amelia is known as."

Amelia is known as "CBS" around school because she's the official broadcasting system. There's a joke that if you want something to be spread around, you don't telegraph, you don't telephone—you tell Amelia.

What R. G. and Dannalee were implying was that Jordan had told Amelia, knowing it would get to me.

"Susu *made* him do it," I said.

Dannalee stared at me. "How come this big defense of Jordan all of a sudden?"

My face flamed. My big, fat, tattletale face.

"She's his campaign manager. He does what she says."

Dannalee's eyes narrowed. I wondered if she guessed how I felt about Jordan. How would she and R. G. feel if they knew I didn't even want to win the election?

It *was* peculiar, as Dad said.

Dannalee looked as if she was going to say something. But before she could, R. G. went on.

Holding up a fourth finger, he said, "He mentioned that slip of the tongue on Friday, just to remind you of your embarrassment. And fifth, he tried to get you to spill the secret campaign promise." R. G. held up all five fingers.

I could have held up a sixth finger. He had dangled a carrot in front of me, in the form of a possible future date.

But *surely* Susu had engineered the whole thing. I could picture him reluctantly agreeing to do it since he was so eager to win. He was innocent.

Still, what he had done was not quite right. Maybe to get even I would really get serious about my campaign, just to scare him a little. Licking a yellow sticker, I smashed it against a foil-wrapped penny with my thumb.

"I'll tell Susu that Snyde ate the candy she brought," I said. Just so I wouldn't be a liar, I unwrapped one of the elderly chews she had brought and tossed it to Snyde, who was still grieving over Marv's rejection that afternoon.

Snyde gummed the chew around a while and then let it drop on the floor, looking up at me with accusing eyes.

"Hey," R. G. said, "did you say Jordan remembered that Marv used to call Snyde 'Aunt Beulah'?"

He and Dannalee had thought Snyde's performance

while Jordan was there had been hilarious, as I told it. "Yes," I said. "He asked if this was the same dog."

"Do you still have the wig Marv used to put on Snyde?" R. G. asked.

"Sure, I think it's around somewhere. Why?"

"Snyde's going to play a part in your campaign."

"He already has," I said glumly. "Remember Susu's drawings?"

"If Jordan remembered 'Aunt Beulah,' the other kids will remember, too," R. G. said. "You'll attract a lot of attention if you have Aunt Beulah riding around with you tomorrow."

It seemed like a good idea until I thought of something.

"What about Traxler? He threatened to jail Snyde and run us out of town if we brought him to Pratt again."

"Traxler will never see him," R. G. said. "We'll take the back way to school and I'll put Snyde in the woodworking shop when we're not using him. Nothing can happen."

R. G. came in Belch to get Snyde and me and my treasure chest the next morning. He had washed the car and polished and shined the chrome so that it looked as good as Belch could look. At the last minute, I took along the bag of stale candy, throwing it on the floor in the back and commenting to R. G. that we could toss it in the river on the way.

"Or use it for missiles if we run into a herd of wild Martians," he said.

When we got to Dannalee's place, she stashed her posters in back with Snyde and me and then crawled in beside R. G. "It's such a gorgeous day that nothing can go wrong," she said.

She was wearing a bag of some kind that day. At least,

that's what it looked like. Sort of a gunnysack with holes cut in it for her head and arms. Over that she wore her shawl. Strangely enough, on her it all looked good.

We started off with the top down. Snyde loved the wind blowing in his ears.

Belch was its usual cranky self, but it managed to lurch us all the way to Pratt.

We weren't a bit prepared for what we saw when we got to the campus.

12

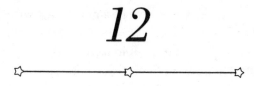

I'VE READ SCIENCE FICTION STORIES about people suddenly finding themselves in an alien world where everything is out of proportion. Looking at the campus of Pratt High, I felt as if I had been teleported to that kind of world. Gigantic flowers had sprouted up all over the quad. Not just a few, but dozens. Maybe hundreds. The whole quad was a mass of color.

Those flowers were at least ten feet high and topped by huge, bright-colored blooms. A second look told me that the blooms were balloons. They had to be helium-filled because they floated gracefully in the gentle breeze, attached to earth by long strings which were anchored in the grass.

The effect was enough to short-circuit your optics. What's more, each one of those bright blooms bore the same message: VOTE FOR JORDAN.

How childish my foil-wrapped pennies were. How pathetic. How *embarrassing!*

But even as I cringed in shame about my own efforts,

I couldn't help but cheer for Jordan's. Compared to me and my crew, Jordan was a Maserati racing its engine in the midst of lumbering garbage trucks, an eagle flapping among dumb little sparrows.

R. G. and Dannalee must have been overwhelmed, too, because nobody said a word as we drove into the parking lot. Even Snyde was silent, his ears pricked forward with curiosity.

Then Dannalee sighed. "How tacky," she said weakly.

"Yeah," R. G. said. "Wish we'd thought of it."

I shrank down in the seat. "Maybe we should just go back home."

Dannalee sprang into action, gathering together her posters. "Not after I worked for a week on these things. We're going to put them up even if nobody ever looks at them."

Belch coughed to a stop. "While you two do that," R. G. said, "I'll get Belch decorated and fix the shelf on the top of the backseat. Then I'll take Snyde and the treasure chest to the woodworking shop until noon."

I don't know how other schools do it, but at Pratt High we always have a parade of candidates and a rally at the football field on the first day of campaigning. Nobody ever does much of anything except just straggle across the quad with signs and things. That's why Jordan's efforts were so unusual. And so intimidating. I had thought I could compete with his show with my treasure chest idea, but now it all seemed kind of pitiful.

As Dannalee and I walked onto the campus, we saw that the candidates who lived in Pratt had already taken the best spots to display their posters. Jordan and Susu and their crew must have gotten there first of all that morning, because blown-up photographs of Jordan's face smiled at us from the prime locations, like the Pratt High sign in front of the administration building and the steps of the gym. There wasn't any printing on the posters. Just his face. He didn't need any printing, not with all those bobbing balloons advertising VOTE FOR JORDAN. We noticed that on each balloon were several of the thumbprint-sized photos like the one Jordan had pasted on my hand on Saturday. Those little photos were everywhere—on the doors, on the trophy case, on lockers.

"It's going to be hard to find a place to put these posters," Dannalee said, "unless we plaster some over Jordan's dumb face."

Dannalee's posters were at least one thing to be proud of. She had used all the ideas we had come up with at our meeting, plus several of her own. They were all done in bright, clear colors. I especially liked the one showing me holding back a mountain of "mystery meat" depicted by an ancient horse, a skinny goat, and several other unidentifiable creatures crawling out of hamburger buns. That was to show I was going to try to improve the food in the cafeteria. Another showed me pouring money into the junior-class treasury, and another had me cracking a PSAT exam. The last one in the series said, "The best is in the chest," and showed me opening up the treasure chest.

Across the bottom of each poster were the words TRISH FOR PRESIDENT, along with a little logo of the chest.

"I wish I knew what I'm going to reveal in that chest," I told Dannalee as we looked for places to tape the posters.

"Why worry? You have until Thursday to figure that out. We have more urgent problems right now." She stopped beside the door to the psychology room. "Here's a good place to put a poster. Most of the sophomores will be coming here sometime today."

We taped up the first poster and were putting down some of the big red footprints that were to lead to the next poster when Dannalee stiffened. "Hey," she said, "that's not fair."

My eyes followed her pointing finger. On the other side of the psychology room door was a poster-sized blowup of the picture Riley McQuaid had taken of R. G. and Snyde and me in the back of Traxler's cop car. Our faces were almost life-sized, and we looked much worse than in the smaller version.

"But we got that picture from Mr. Anderson at the photo shop," I sputtered.

"We didn't get the negative. Riley had that." Dannalee marched forward and ripped the picture from the wall, tearing it down the middle. "There are probably others around, but we don't have time to look for them right now." She handed me the torn picture. "Get rid of this, then go to class. Tell Ms. Evans I'll be a little late."

"What are you going to do?"

"Don't ask," Dannalee said over her shoulder as she hurried down the hall. "I'll get the rest of the posters put up, so don't worry about them."

I ditched the torn picture in a wastecan and went to class. Dannalee never did show up for it.

Snyde was sitting in Belch's front seat wearing his Aunt Beulah wig when I got to the parking lot at noon. R. G. had draped VOTE FOR TRISH banners on each side of Belch. Dannalee had made them from some of her mother's old sheets, and they looked homemade but okay.

My treasure chest was already installed on its shelf on

top of Belch's backseat, along with a sign that said, "The best is in the chest."

A lot of Wolf Creek kids were standing around waiting to march in my little parade. The only person who wasn't there was Dannalee.

On the other side of the parking lot, Jordan's marching band was tuning up with "Cheer, Cheer for Noble Pratt High," and I could hear Jordan saying something over a bullhorn.

"We don't have any music," I said to R. G. "I'd like you to lead this show with your tuba."

R. G. looked doubtful. "Just me and my tuba? Won't that look pretty silly?"

"Think about it, R. G. We're not exactly a class act. Your tuba would fit right in with everything else."

R. G. surveyed Belch with our homemade banners and Snyde sitting there in his curly blond wig. Grinning, he said, "I think you have a good idea there."

Commandeering Gordie Coons to drive Belch, he pulled his tuba from the backseat and began blowing into it.

Dannalee swooped in just before we started our little parade, looking very pleased with herself.

"Sorry I couldn't let you help," she said, "but I didn't want you disqualified at the last minute for cutting classes."

I didn't have time to ask her what she had been up to because Gordie Coons had Belch's engine clattering away and we were ready to move. I scrambled up to my perch beside my treasure chest, and we were off to join the rest of the candidates. At the last minute, Dannalee ran up and draped the shawl she had worn that day around Snyde, adding to his Aunt Beulah image.

The parade started off with the ASB candidates. None

of them did much of anything except march along with banners and flags, except for Steve Colby. Steve is on the football team, and he had a bunch of cheerleaders leading cheers from the back of a flatbed truck.

The senior-class candidates were next. One of them had some kids unroll a banner that was almost as long as the quad.

Jordan's group was next. His cheering section, dressed in blue and white and led by Susu, were throwing things to the crowd—candy kisses and those miniature Hershey bars. One of the guys was throwing something that looked suspiciously like the stale candy chews Susu had given me. Looking down on the floor where I had put the bag of candy, I saw that it was gone.

I turned around to look at Dannalee. "Is that what I think it is?" I asked, pointing.

She nodded happily. "I bribed somebody for a supply of his little thumbprint pictures, and I pasted one on every piece."

I couldn't help grinning, although I wished it had been Susu's face on that poisonous candy.

We were moving across the quad now. Right ahead of us Jordan's band was playing, "We're loyal to you, Pratt High; To honor you we'll ever try. . . ." Jordan was standing on his little "campaign platform" with his arms raised in a wide V for victory. He was wearing white pants, a blue shirt, and a white vest, all coordinated with his supporters and the decorations on his platform. That was the key word of his whole show—*coordinated*.

If my group had a key word it would had to have been *slapdash*. But R. G. tooted his tuba in beat with Jordan's band, Belch got into the rhythm of things with a lurch, lurch,

lurch, and Snyde punctuated the music with joyful barks. Dannalee was walking alongside yelling, "Aunt Beulah votes for Trish." I clung to my perch atop Belch's backseat with one hand and waved with the other. Behind me the other Wolf Creekers carried signs that said "Trish for Junior-Class President" and flung the foil-wrapped pennies.

All in all, we attracted a lot of attention. At least we gave everybody a good laugh. One guy yelled, "When are you going to show us your chest, Trish?" and I just grinned and waved.

To tell the truth, I liked it. It was fun having people look up at me and other people yell my name. It was exciting seeing the TRISH FOR PRESIDENT posters all around the quad. I saw that what Dannalee had done was to put one of my posters up near each of Jordan's, then put big red footprints leading up to them so that my posters were the most noticeable.

There was a little delay between the parade and the rally because the students had to run the short distance from the quad to the football bleachers. A lot of the kids stopped to greet "Aunt Beulah" as they went past, and some even said, "Great show, Trish."

We passed in front of the bleachers in the same order as we paraded across the quad, so we were behind Jordan again, making the most of his band. His crew stopped in front of the bleachers and gave a little demonstration.

"Give us a J," his supporters shouted, "give us an O, give us an R, give us a D, give us an A, give us an N. *Give us Jordan!*" they screamed.

Jordan stood there beaming, his arms still raised for victory. The hail of stale candy caught him completely by surprise. Some of the chews had been opened and partially eaten, and a couple of them stuck to his clothing.

"*Give us a bellyache*," somebody yelled, and there was a lot of laughter.

I turned to Dannalee. "Did you tell them to do that?" I demanded.

She grinned with delight. "No, I didn't, but I would have if I had thought of it."

I looked at Jordan. I wanted to call out that the stale candy wasn't his fault. I wanted to tell the kids to stop throwing it.

But Jordan knew how to save the situation. Exchanging his bewildered look for a grin, he yelled, "I'll give you a lot more than a bellyache. I'll give you *good student government!*"

His backers cheered as they moved off down the field.

My little caravan took the spot front and center. R. G. *oompah-pah*ed in time with Jordan's band. Snyde barked. I waved.

And Belch died.

That was the signal for everything to go wrong. Jordan's band gave a final blast and stopped, leaving R. G.'s *oompah*s hanging in the air like forlorn bleats of a lost billy goat. Snyde saw a curious cat at the edge of the field and hurtled from the car, tripping and stumbling over Dannalee's shawl but managing to keep his wig in place. Over in Jordan's part of the world I heard Susu screeching, "He's *dangerous!*"

That should have been the moment for Traxler to show up, but this time he didn't. We were in luck.

Nobody was doing anything, so I took over.

"R. G.," I said, "keep playing while we move over to

our assigned spot. You guys"—I pointed to some of the Wolf Creekers—"you push Belch right behind him. Dannalee, you go get Snyde. He knows you."

Everybody began to obey my orders. It all worked out smoothly, as if it were part of our show. Everybody cheered when Dannalee brought "Aunt Beulah" back. And I had a taste of what it was like to wield power. A person could get to like it.

We never did get Belch started again. R. G. got the Wolf Creekers to push it to the parking lot after the rally, and that's were it stayed, looking sad and abandoned with the VOTE FOR TRISH banners still draped across its sides.

I had a little run-in with Susu as we all went back to classes.

"You think you're smart, don't you?" she gritted at me as she passed on the quad. "Well, it's not over yet."

And it wasn't. There were more blown-up pictures of me around the campus. One was of me and Snyde in our manure-spattered truck on the day Susu thought he attacked her. Another was of me falling off the platform on the day of the introductions.

But they didn't bother me much anymore. I had gotten the most cheers at the rally, and I was feeling mighty mellow.

We had to take Snyde home on the school bus, which didn't please Lester very much. We left his blond wig on and told Lester he was a new girl in town, but Lester didn't think it was funny.

"I'm not supposed to allow animals on this bus," he complained.

But when R. G. told him Snyde was going to help me win the election, Lester allowed him to come aboard.

Snyde and I shared a seat and Dannalee sat with R. G. That was a bit of a downer, but I sat and entertained myself thinking about how it would be to actually *be* president of the junior class. I could give Jordan some job so that we would be working together, and everything would still work out all right.

Dannalee reminded me that we had arranged to have her mother help me with my assembly speech for Thursday. I asked R. G. if he would see that Snyde got home and he said he would, so I got off the bus with Dannalee.

Dannalee's mother met us at the door with a smile as broad as a rainbow.

"Guess what?" she sang.

There was only one thing that could make her that happy.

"You sold a story," Dannalee and I said together.

"I did, I did, I surely did," Mrs. Davis chortled.

I guess good things were being passed out all over that day.

13

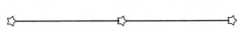

DANNALEE AND I GRABBED MRS. DAVIS, and the three of us danced around the room. I had never seen Mrs. Davis so excited. You could have fried hamburgers in the bright glow from her face.

Even jumping for joy wears a person out, and eventually we all dropped breathless onto chairs.

Mrs. Davis fanned herself with her hands. "I've been twitching around here by myself ever since the mail came. I couldn't wait to tell somebody."

"Doesn't Daddy know yet?" Dannalee asked.

Her mother shook her head. "He's been at Bill Pickett's all day fixing the tractor. I could have phoned him, but I guess I needed warm bodies here to jump up and down with me." Mrs. Davis waved the letter above her head. "Can you believe it? I sold a story. I, little old Norma Davis, *sold a story!*"

That wasn't like her at all. She was always putting herself down, saying what a loser she was as a housekeeper and how she could win a prize as Mrs. Indigestion of the Year with her cooking. Now she was almost breaking her arm to give herself a pat on the back.

She couldn't sit still. Leaping to her feet, she did a couple more pirouettes around the room. "I'm an *author*," she sang.

Dannalee sat forward on her chair. "You've been an author for years, Mom. What about all those other things you've written?"

"Oh, those." Mrs. Davis stopped dancing and looked at the neatly stacked boxes of manuscripts in the utility room. "Okay, I guess *I* knew I was an author. But now somebody else recognizes me as one. And they're willing to *pay* me for my work. I guess that makes a difference."

I hadn't even thought about the pay part. Neither had Dannalee, because she said, "*Money!* Oh, wow, Mom, is there a check in the letter?"

"No," Mrs. Davis said. "They just say they'll be sending it right along. Here, look." She handed the letter to Dannalee.

"Dear Mrs. Davis," Dannalee read. "All of us here like your story, 'The Mortgage Is Due at Six.' " She looked up at her mother. " 'The Mortgage Is Due at Six'?"

Mrs. Davis seemed a little self-conscious. "Oh, it's just a little story about a woman who spends her house payment on some clothes, and then what she does about it."

Dannalee looked back at the letter and then vaulted off her chair. "One thousand dollars! Trish, are my eyes seeing right?" She came over to hold the letter in front of my eyes, jabbing at the words with her finger.

Sure enough, it said one thousand dollars. The letter was from the editor of a magazine I saw on the newsstand at Johnson's Drugstore in Pratt all the time. The return address was New York, New York.

"Wow, Mrs. Davis. You're a celebrity!" I thought of all the years I had seen her hunched over her typewriter out there in the utility room, all the years when people said she ought to be scrubbing her house or canning peaches or doing something useful. I wondered what they would say now.

"My lands, I'm no celebrity." Mrs. Davis blushed a little. "I'm really sort of embarrassed to think of all that money just for my little story."

"Evidently those people in New York think you're worth it, Mom. *One thousand dollars!*" Dannalee pretended to faint onto a chair. "And it wasn't even one of your sizzling romances. Aren't there *any* kissy scenes in it? No rich doctor flying in to rescue the maiden in distress?"

"Well," Mrs. Davis said, "there's a nice scene with her husband at the end. But the woman solves her own problem." She *hmmmm*ed thoughtfully. "Maybe that's what makes it different from my other stories."

Dannalee leaped up and planted a big kiss on her mother's cheek. "My mother, the author!"

"Congratulations, Mrs. Davis," I said.

She smiled at both of us. "You girls make me feel so good. Oh, but here I've been blabbing on about *me* when you came for help on your speech. I haven't got the sense of a turtle. I should have asked right off how *your* day went. Did everything go the way you planned?"

Dannalee and I both laughed. "Not exactly," I said. "But it worked out okay."

Dannalee nodded. "Trish is beginning to see herself as a real live candidate."

As Dannalee told what had happened that day, I wondered if I was seeing myself differently because *other* people were beginning to see me as a serious candidate, because *Jordan* was thinking of me as somebody important. Maybe it was like Mrs. Davis said, that you need a worthwhile image reflected back from somebody else before you can really believe in yourself.

Dannalee's father came into the house while she was still telling her mother about what a hit Snyde had been as "Aunt Beulah."

"I thought there must be a party going on here," Mr. Davis said. "I could hear hollering and laughing clear out by the front gate."

"Daddy," Dannalee said, "come in and hear the good news."

Mr. Davis wiped his feet on a little rag rug before coming into the living room. "I could use some good news. Maybe I'd best clean up first." He looked down at his blue denim overalls, which were covered with dirt and grease. He seemed tired. "Been fighting with that tractor again. The damned thing doesn't want to go."

"Harry." Mrs. Davis' eyes sparkled. "You can go ahead and order the new parts you need for it."

"Last time I heard, you had to have money to do that." Mr. Davis rubbed his greasy hands together. "Lay the good news on me, Dannalee, and I'll go scrape off some of this muck." He looked around at all of us, waiting.

"Tell him, Mom," Dannalee urged.

"Harry, I sold a story." Mrs. Davis' voice was kind of high and excited.

"A story?" Mr. Davis looked puzzled. "One of those little yarns you're always typing away on?"

Mrs. Davis nodded. "I *sold* one. To a magazine."

"Well, that's right fine." Without touching her with his greasy hands, Mr. Davis leaned over to give her a peck on the cheek. "Glad to hear it. Maybe that will help you get it out of your system." He started toward the hallway that led to the bathroom. "I better get cleaned up before I get somebody all dirty."

Mrs. Davis reached up and took hold of her husband's face with one hand, turning it back so he had to look at her.

"Harry," she said, "read my lips. I *sold* a story. They're paying me *money*. You can go ahead and order those tractor parts."

Mr. Davis' mouth was pinched sideways by his wife's grip on his face, but he tried to give her a patient smile. "It isn't some two-bit bolts I need, Norma. Those parts come to four, maybe five hundred dollars."

Letting go of his face, Mrs. Davis took her letter from Dannalee and held it up so Mr. Davis could see it. Squinting, he read it.

"Well, I'll be twanged," he said. "They mean that? A thousand dollars just for one of those little stories of yours?"

Mrs. Davis nodded. "So get on the phone and order those parts."

"Aw, shoot, Norma, a man can't take money from his wife."

"I've been taking money from you all these years."

"But a man's got his pride to think about, Norma."

Mrs. Davis quivered a little, as if she were standing on a bowl of Jell-O. "Harry," she said. Her voice was rough. "A woman's got pride, too, Harry."

He stood there looking down at her. It was like watching a play, and I waited to see what he was going to say. As

132

the seconds clicked by, I found myself holding my breath. *Oh, let him say the right thing,* I prayed.

Finally he spoke. "I'll do it, Norma. I'll order those parts. And I do thank you." Suddenly he grabbed her and swung her high off her feet. "Whooo-*eee*," he yelled. "I got me a woman who's really something!" Setting her down, he said, "Go get yourself gussied up and we'll go to Pratt and have dinner at the Upstairs Cafe. Is there a movie at the Grand that a man can take his wife to for a celebration?"

Dannalee was jittering up and down. "You go get ready, too, Daddy. I'll take care of the cows and all. You and Mom go live it up."

"I can't leave you to do a man's work, Dannalee," Mr. Davis protested.

"I've been working right alongside you for years," Dannalee said. "Haven't you noticed? Now, go." She pushed them both toward the hall door.

"I'll help her, Mr. Davis," I offered.

"Hell of a note," he grumbled. "Being bossed around by a bunch of women." Grinning, he put his arm around his wife's shoulders. "I never believed all that scribbling of yours could amount to anything, Norma."

"I know you didn't, Harry."

Mr. Davis shrugged. "A man can be wrong."

"He sure can," Mrs. Davis said.

Mr. Davis looked down at her. "But *I'm* paying for this party tonight."

Mrs. Davis gave him a radiant smile. "That's right sweet of you, Harry."

"A man can't give up *all* his rights." As they started down the hall, Mr. Davis whistled through his teeth. "Whoo-*eee*! A *thousand* dollars. Whooo-*eee*!"

133

Dannalee breathed a sigh of relief as she watched them go. "Wow, I was really scared there for a minute or two. My dad could have wiped Mom out with a couple of words."

"Yeah," I agreed. I wondered if I would have the courage to face that kind of scene. What if Jordan wouldn't like it if I decided to be a career woman? For some reason I thought of Blaine saying he wanted my sister always to be his little homecoming queen. She seemed happy enough to be just that. But maybe there wasn't anything else she had wanted to be. Then there was Mrs. Toomey. What about her?

"You know," Dannalee was saying, "it's really funny how the sale of one story turned my mother into such a tiger. I really think she might have packed up and left if my dad had wiped her out."

"Yeah," I agreed. "Her writing really means a lot to her."

Dannalee began moving around the room, straightening sofa pillows and picking up newspapers. "I don't think anything's going to stop my mom now," she said thoughtfully. "I hope my dad's the kind who can live with a woman who might make more money than he does."

"Good grief, Dannalee, do you think he might *not* be?"

Dannalee looked a little worried. "He might be. But hey, he loves her, I know that. And they both have a great sense of humor. So I guess my dad isn't going to take his new tractor parts and split."

I knew Dannalee felt as relieved as I did about that decision. I picked up some newspapers and stacked them neatly on an end table. "Dannalee, do you think that if a person wants another person to think of her in a way that's different from the way the other person sees her, do you think the person can overdo it and scare the other person away for good?"

Dannalee looked blank. "Run that by me again."

"Forget I said it." I turned away from Dannalee's narrowed eyes. If I didn't watch it, she was going to guess how I felt about Jordan and why I was running for class president and the whole thing. And suddenly I wasn't very proud of it. What if I twisted myself around to be what Jordan wanted me to be and found that I didn't like myself that way? Couldn't he love me the way *I* wanted to be?

I formulated a future scene in my mind. Jordan would be saying, "I thought I loved you before, but it was nothing to what I think of you now, Madam President."

"Oh, Jordan," I would whisper, and then I would bend my head and kiss him.

No, no, that was all wrong. *He* was supposed to bend *his* head and kiss *me*.

But how was Jordan going to feel if things kept going well for me and I won? Right now he was seeing me as the kind of girl he'd like to take out. Wasn't that what I wanted? Shouldn't I quit while I was ahead?

To break off my thoughts, I called my mom to tell her I was staying to help Dannalee with the chores. "Tell Dad I may be late," I said.

"Don't worry, Trish," Mom told me. "He can handle things."

I grinned into the phone. "I know he can, Mom. Bye."

Dannalee's parents came out looking really spiffy. "We'll be off now," Mrs. Davis said. "I guess you girls can find something to eat."

"Mom," Dannalee said, "go."

Mrs. Davis laughed. "I guess that's really a dumb worry

after all the nights I've typed right through dinnertime while *you* cooked."

"No guilt trips, Mom." Dannalee shooed them out the door. "Enjoy your big evening, *author!*"

We stood in the doorway and watched them drive away.

"You know," Dannalee said, "I'll never admit it to her, but I did used to resent all the time she spent at her typewriter. I think Sarabeth and Raylene did, too."

"But what about all those school plays and things? You said you were proud of her for those."

Dannalee sighed and turned back into the house. "I always liked those things just fine. But I wanted the homemade-cookie routine and everything. I wanted my house to look like yours when I got home from school, with the nice snack waiting and your mom asking what happened that day. My mom was usually typing away and telling me to save it till later."

"That's kind of funny," I said. "I was always envying the way *your* mom spent so much time teaching us to give speeches and do plays and stuff." I didn't mention that sometimes I had felt sorry for Dannalee because she had had to get dinner ready.

Dannalee grinned. "So I guess a person can't have everything. Trish, what kind of mom are you going to be when you have kids? I mean, are you going to be a cookie mom or a do-your-own-thing mom?"

I didn't want to talk about that right then. "I don't know, Dannalee. But I do know that I came here to write my assembly speech. If we don't get to it, the election will be over before I figure out a single word to say."

14

"TRISH," DANNALEE SAID, "I'm not good at writing speeches. Maybe we'd just better wait until tomorrow night when my mom can help us. She'll probably have come back to earth by then."

"Well, I'm getting a little worried about it since our time is running out. Let's just figure out in general what I'm going to say."

Dannalee tapped her lips with a forefinger. "You won't need to say a whole lot since most of the time will be spent talking about your secret campaign promise when you open your treasure chest. Do you know what your secret campaign promise is yet?"

I drooped. "No. I'm expecting it to show up in a blinding flash of inspiration."

"I read about a lady who had a blinding flash of inspiration once," Dannalee said. "She said she learned that the world rests on the back of a duck, and every time it quacks we have a thunderstorm."

"Dannalee, you're making that up."

"I'll be glad to make up your speech, too."

"I guess you're right. I'd better wait and have your mom help me."

Dannalee was rolling now. "Your secret campaign promise could be that you'll give out kisses to the football team under the gym stairs every Thursday."

"Dannalee!"

"It would get you a lot of votes."

I didn't have to answer that because the phone rang. Dannalee answered it.

"Oh, hi, R. G.," she said. "Yes, Trish is still here."

I was surprised by the stab of jealousy that sliced through me. I thought I had settled the problem of Dannalee and R. G. in my mind. It wasn't any of my business if he called her up. He probably wanted to come over as soon as I cleared out of the way. Then he and Dannalee could have the house to themselves until her folks came home. To do what? Had she kissed him yet? That mouth that she thought was the most kissable mouth of any guy we knew? Had she been pulled up against his rock-hard chest?

Why should I care?

I *did* care.

"Okay, R. G.," Dannalee was saying. "We'll see you then." She hung up the phone. "R. G.'s coming right over. He wants to talk to you."

To *me*! I was ashamed at how relieved I was that they weren't kicking me out so they could be alone.

We heard R. G.'s tuba long before we saw him loping across the fields. He was playing what must have been the tuba part to some fast march music.

As the *oompah-pahs* got louder, Dannalee and I scurried around the kitchen locating some food. R. G.'s first words were going to be something like "What have you got to eat?" What we had was some cheese and crackers and rather withered winter apples. We had them already spread out on the table when R. G. burst through the door with a final blat of his tuba.

R. G.'s eyes lit up when he saw the meager rations we had found. "I'm starving," he said and then went on. "I've got an idea to help keep interest up in your campaign for the next couple of days, Trish."

Dannalee took the tuba from his hands and pushed him gently down onto a chair. "Before you start on that, let me tell you some good news." She motioned for me to sit down and began passing around the cheese and crackers. "My mom sold a story, R. G."

A big grin spread across R. G.'s face as she told him the details.

"I always knew your mom could do it," he said. "Our town should be really proud of her. Not many places the size of Wolf Creek have an author in residence."

" 'Author in residence,' " Dannalee repeated. "That sounds impressive."

"It *is* impressive. Your mom will put Wolf Creek on the map." R. G. stuffed cheese and crackers into his mouth and chewed.

"Want to bet some people will still say she should have tended to her duties?" Dannalee asked.

We all laughed.

"She's a great mom, and don't forget it," R. G. said.

I thought about R. G.'s mom being dead. Dannalee and I were really lucky still to have ours.

"Why would I forget it?" Dannalee asked. "Hey, R. G.,

you didn't come over here to talk about moms. Why don't you tell us this big-deal idea of yours?"

R. G. swallowed his cheese and crackers. "Okay, this is what it is. I want to donate Belch to the campaign."

"Donate Belch?" I was puzzled. "But I thought Belch was as good as dead and buried after the parade today."

"I know what we're going to do," Dannalee said. "We're going to name it the official pace car for the Jordan Avery Presidential Race."

"Not quite," R. G. said. "We're going to have a car bash. Three bashes for a buck, with the money going to the junior-class treasury, no matter who wins the election."

Dannalee and I gasped in unison.

"*Bash* Belch?" Dannalee said.

"Like hit it with hammers?" I asked.

"Sledgehammers." R. G. concentrated on biting into one of the withered apples. It collapsed under his teeth like a rubber ball. "I had Mr. Cramer from my automotive class look it over. He said it's really thrashed and would take a bundle to fix up. So I want to put it to good use. The kids are all wondering what we're going to do next, Trish, so tomorrow we'll put up signs telling about the big car bash on Thursday, just before the election assembly."

"But you love Belch," I protested. "I mean, you're a twosome. How can you wreck it? Would Romeo go around bashing Juliet?"

R. G. wouldn't look at me. "If I get rid of it, I'll save a lot more money for college. Look, I'll get the permission slips and all that tomorrow. We'll have a couple of days to build up enthusiasm. On Thursday we'll have the bash, then go on to the assembly where we'll have Aunt Beulah and the treasure chest. You can zap them with the best speech of your career, and we'll leave Jordan and Susu wondering what happened."

"Wait a minute." R. G. was moving too fast for me. "What's this about Aunt Beulah? I'm not taking Snyde into Pratt again. It was just pure luck that Traxler didn't show up today. I'm not going to stretch it for another day."

"I've got everything planned." R. G. reached for the last piece of cheese. "We'll hide Snyde the way we did today. We'll whisk him out of town right after school. What could go wrong?"

We made up the posters we would need to announce the bash, and then R. G. helped Dannalee and me with the cows and other chores. It was getting dark by the time he and I started walking home. We cut across the fields because it was the shorter route.

"R. G.," I said. Our feet crushed the young alfalfa as we walked, and the smell of that combined with the scent of apple blossoms from the orchards around us was enough to put me on some kind of high. "R. G., I thought we were going to deal with the issues in my campaign. Now we're getting into the showy stuff, like car bashes and all the kinds of things that Jordan does."

"So what are you worried about, Trish? Seems to me we're doing pretty well."

I couldn't tell him I was worried about maybe doing *too* well. I couldn't say I wasn't sure I wanted to take a chance on actually *winning* the election. "Well, I just thought our strategy was going to be to stick to the issues."

"You have to change the strategy to fit the battle," R. G. said. "If you stand around talking about how to increase PSAT scores while Jordan shoots off fireworks, who's going to listen to you?" Putting his tuba to his lips, he blew a blast that flushed a sleepy owl from its perch in a choke-cherry tree. It swooped off, *whoo-whooing*. "You're going to win this election, Trish. And you're going to be the best president a junior class ever had." Soft moonlight touched his nice face as he looked down at me.

Sudden hot tears filled my eyes. Why was I so anxious to get Jordan to see me as a worthwhile person when R. G. had never seen me as anything else? R. G. saw strengths in me that I didn't even know I had, and he encouraged me to make the most of them. With a guy like R. G. I could be a homebody if that's what I wanted to be, or I could be a career woman if *that's* what I wanted to be. Or if I decided to try to do both, a guy like R. G. would break his back to help me.

We stood there in the field looking at one another. For just a minute, I thought he was going to drop his tuba and take me into his arms. Crazy me, I wanted him to. I wanted him to hold me close while I sobbed out how mixed-up I was about everything, how unworthy I was of his trust, how I wished we could be little kids again when things weren't so complicated.

But R. G. didn't drop his tuba, and I couldn't just fling myself into his arms. It would only embarrass him, and me, too. Besides, he liked Dannalee.

I sniffed back my tears before they could start, and we began walking again. R. G. was talking about how he'd have to get a big tarp for Belch to sit on while we bashed it so its parts wouldn't litter the parking lot.

Then, after he said good night, I listened to the mournful *oompah* of his tuba grow fainter and fainter as he walked away from me in the moonlit, apple-blossom night.

Dad was just letting the cows out of the barn after milking, so I knew he was already through with most of the chores. I went into the house, where I found Mom working on her genealogy with her pedigree and family-group sheets spread around the kitchen table.

"Hi, Mom," I said. "Did Snyde get home all right?" I had forgotten to ask R. G. about him.

"Oh, sure." Mom reached out to give my arm a welcoming pat. "R. G. brought him home."

Just then the telephone rang, so I went to answer it. It was Marv, calling from his dorm at the university.

"Trish," he said, "how's it going?"

"Okay. How are you, Marv? Did you want to talk to Mom?"

"I wanted to talk to you, Trish." Marv cleared his throat. "Trish, I just wanted to say I'm sorry about Sunday."

"About Sunday?" I tried to replay Sunday. "What about Sunday?"

"Well, you know. Susu. I kind of saw her in a new light on Sunday. She's out to get you."

"So what's new, Marv? Susu's been out to get people ever since she was three hours old."

"Okay, so I'm a little dense. I don't know why I ever thought she was such a fox."

"I don't either, Marv."

"Hey, Trish, you're not making it any easier. I've had to swallow my pride to make this phone call. I guess I should have made it last night before you used that dumb candy she brought you."

My hand tightened on the receiver. "I didn't use it. I've got a few smarts, Marv."

"Okay, don't get all bent out of shape. I'm only trying to help. What I wanted to tell you is that I think you should get out of that election. Let Jordan have it. You're playing with barracudas with that bunch. They'll eat you alive."

"I'm doing all right, Marv."

"Trish, believe Big Brother. When you play with barracudas, you have to do as the barracudas do. You're not made of that kind of stuff."

Wasn't I? Maybe not. On the other hand, Marv had never seen me the way I really was. Or the way I *thought* I was. Maybe that was why I had to try so hard to do the same work he did at home. To prove I was his equal.

"If it were you running in this election," I said, "would you stay with it?"

"Of course I would. I could handle it."

"I can handle it, too, Marv."

The phone line hummed while I waited for Marv to say something. He cleared his throat again. "Well, then, I guess all I can do is wish you well."

"Thanks, Marv. I can use a few good wishes."

The line hummed again, then Marv said, "You know, Trish, maybe I should get to know you better."

Maybe I should get to know myself better, I thought after he hung up. One part of me wanted to get out and prove to Marv and everybody else that I could face the world and fight those barracudas. Another part just wanted to cook dinner for Jordan every night.

Who *was* the real Trish?

15

"WHAT WAS MARV CALLING ABOUT?" Mom asked.

I sat down across from her at the kitchen table. "He just wanted to wish me well in the election."

"R. G. says you're going to win it," Mom said. "He stopped to talk awhile when he brought Snyde home."

"Yeah, he told me I'd win, too." I didn't want to think about how R. G. had so much faith in me when I was such a fraud.

Mom must have heard something in my voice because she said, "Trish? Don't you want to win?"

My first impulse was to say, "Of course I want to win," and then escape upstairs to my room where I could worry about my life the way Mom cooks a stew, throwing everything into the cookpot of my mind and simmering it over the heat of my confusion. Mom wouldn't question me any further if I chose to do that. But she was sitting there now, quietly available if I needed her—the way she had always been available when I needed her. A cookie mom, always there, always ready to listen, always giving.

"Mom," I said, "I'm so mixed-up." I fiddled with her genealogy sheets.

Mom waited.

I didn't know where to start. How could I just blurt out that I was having an identity crisis and part of it was that I didn't think I wanted to be like her? Or maybe I did. How could I tell her I loved Jordan—but had wanted to fling myself into R. G.'s arms a few minutes before?

How could I explain about how I wanted to be tough enough to fight barracudas, yet gentle enough to soothe a child's tears—as she had always done mine?

I was more mixed-up than I thought.

I cleared my throat, not looking at Mom. I couldn't see whether she was looking at me, but suddenly I saw her hands become very busy stacking her genealogy sheets into a neat pile. That's one of Mom's little tricks. If she knows it's hard for you to look her in the eye, she'll do something so that both of you can look at that and not have to sit there eyeball to eyeball.

I reached out and touched one of her sheets. "Am I related to all of these people?"

"Yes," Mom said. She picked up a pedigree sheet. "This is your line of forefathers on my side back to the sixteenth century."

"Forefathers," I said. "What about my fore*mothers*?"

"They're all here, too, Trish. See, here are all the female lines." She pointed.

I read the names. Athena Petersen, my mother's mother. Maren Olsen, mother of my mother's mother. Elsie Bergsen, mother of my mother's mother's mother.

"Just names," I mused. "None of them ever did anything but have babies so there would be more names."

Spots of red showed up high on Mom's cheeks.

"I mean, I've heard what some of my forefathers did. Like the one who pulled a handcart across the plains. And the one who fought in the Civil War. And the Danish sea captain. But all these women were only mothers."

I should have bitten off my tongue before saying such a thing.

"Trish." Mom's voice was calm, but I wondered if she would have liked to slap my silly face. "Trish, there's not much of anything in the whole world more important than being a good mother and bringing up a fine family. That's what keeps our civilization going. Some of these mothers were pretty heroic, making homes in wildernesses under all kinds of conditions."

I sputtered a little, trying to find something to say that wouldn't make things worse.

"As for not doing anything else," Mom went on, "who do you think made the lovely old quilt on your bed? Your great grandmother was a farm wife with more work than she had time for, but she was known all over this part of the country for her fabulous quilts." She pointed to a name. Blaney Elder. "This woman was a midwife. Birthed almost every baby in the valley when it was first settled. And this one." She pointed to Selena Blake. "She was a suffragette. Used to stump all over the state giving speeches. You might have gotten your speech-making talent from her."

"The next sound you hear," I said, "will be the noise of a big, fat foot being pulled out of a big, fat mouth."

The glowing spots on Mom's cheeks faded a little. "Didn't mean to climb on my soapbox. But, Trish, there are whole lifetimes behind every one of these names. Some of them *were* just homemakers, but the homemaking arts are what make life pleasant and good. Besides, a lot of them didn't have the choices you do as to what they would do with their lives." She eyed me closely. "What brought all this on, anyway?"

I shrugged. "I don't know, Mom. I guess I'm a little confused right now about all those choices. I don't know whether I should really be running for office and preparing for a career or just thinking about settling down, the way Gloria did. You said one day that you wished you had done more with your life, Mom. I guess I keep thinking I should do as much as I can with mine."

"Do you think I've been unhappy being a wife and mother, Trish?"

I was beginning to feel miserable. The light spilling over the table from the big white bulb overhead seemed too bright for my eyes.

"I guess it depends on what you had to give up to do it," I mumbled. "Like Mrs. Toomey—she had to give up her violin."

Mom nodded. "But have you ever watched her face when she talks about those seven fine children of hers? I guess there's a price for success in any field, Trish."

I thought about Dannalee's mother and the price she had paid for her success.

"Oh, hey, Mom," I said, "Mrs. Davis sold a story to a magazine in New York."

Mom's smile was wide. "Oh, now, isn't that grand! She's been working at that for such a long time. She has a whole lot of talent."

"So do you, Mom."

"Thanks." Mom put her hand over mine. "I don't know what's best for you, Trish. You'll have to decide for yourself. Maybe having such a wide choice just makes it harder. Some women do a great job of combining homemaking and careers."

"I know. Maybe that's what I'll do." I stood up. "Did you have to give up something to be such a success at momming, Mom?"

Mom thought about it. "I have no regrets, Trish."

I patted Mom's pile of genealogy sheets. "Well, I've learned one thing today, and it's that I come from a long line of gallant women." Picking up my books, I went to my room. I hadn't made any big decisions about what to do with my life, but I did know that I had to fight the barracudas. And I had to try to win. If I lost Jordan in the process, maybe that was the price of my success.

But maybe I wouldn't win.

The next morning I tried not to look at R. G. as he and Dannalee and I trotted around the campus putting up the signs about the car bash on Thursday before the election assembly. But my eyes kept following his tall, skinny shape as he tacked the signs on poles or taped them to walls. And Dannalee's short, skinny shape was right there beside him.

I should be happy for them, I kept telling myself. *My two best friends in the whole world. I should be very glad they're a twosome.* If Jordan and I got together, we could be a foursome. But somehow I couldn't quite visualize Jordan joining the rest of us. And if he and I *didn't* get together, I would just be a third wheel hanging around with R. G. and Dannalee.

Half a dozen blown-up pictures of Snyde and me appeared in odd places on campus that day, courtesy of Riley McQuaid and Susu, I was sure.

But the pictures backfired. At least three people commented to me that they had seen them and asked if "Aunt Beulah" would be joining me again before the campaign was over. So R. G. was right. We would have to bring Snyde to Pratt once more.

That afternoon I stopped off at Dannalee's again, and her mother helped me put together a neat little speech about the treasures of Pratt High School.

"Since you'll be ending up with something about your secret campaign promise, you'd better decide what it is," Mrs. Davis advised.

"How about having everybody *guess* what it is?" Dannalee suggested. "Tell them the real treasure is in the chest, and then, when they come up with some good guess, say that's what it is."

I liked that. At least it was an alternative to displaying an empty chest. "Thanks for the blinding flash of inspiration, Dannalee."

"Glad you recognize one when it comes along," she said.

I recognized another blinding flash of inspiration the next morning on the school bus when R. G. beckoned Dannalee to come sit by him on one of the seats in the back. The flash told me that the days of our three-sided friendship were over. R. G. and Dannalee didn't need me anymore.

When we got to Pratt High, I went straight to first-period English class. Dannalee caught up with me there.

"Hey, what's the big idea?" she panted. "How come you didn't wait for me?"

"You and R. G. had a lot to talk about. I didn't want

to break it up." I tried to sound light and casual, but I came off like a pouty kid.

"We were just talking about something. You'll find out about it tomorrow."

They were probably going to announce their engagement.

"By the way," Dannalee said, "I won't be going to lunch with you today. You don't mind, do you?"

"Why should I? I can find my way to the lunchroom alone."

Dannalee blinked, and I was sorry I'd been rude. "I mean, who knows, I might find somebody exciting to eat with."

I was just making things worse, so I shut up.

At noon I headed for the lunchroom, alone, after watching Dannalee and R. G. leave the campus together. They were headed uptown. I wasn't spying on them. Yes, I was. It wasn't much fun being dropped so suddenly after we had been such good friends since we were little kids. I didn't like them going off together on their secret, personal business.

I went through the lunch line and headed purposefully toward an empty table. It was uncomfortable being there alone. I thought of barging in on somebody's little group, but decided that would look kind of pushy, like I was just doing it to get their votes.

I was almost to the table when I heard somebody saying my name.

"Trish. Trish."

I looked toward the voice. Jordan! Jordan was sitting alone at a table, and he was calling to me.

"Care to join me, Trish?" he asked.

Who cared if R. G. and Dannalee had deserted me?

"I'd like to, Jordan." I gave him a bright smile that would tell anybody who happened to be looking that we had planned to meet there to talk about the election.

Jordan grinned as I arrived at his table. "It's lonely at the top, isn't it? Nobody came to sit by me, and I kept telling myself it was because they think I'm too busy thinking about my campaign to be bothered."

"Where's Susu?" The words were out before I had time to catch them.

Jordan didn't seem to mind my rudeness. "She's working with a committee on some posters for tomorrow. She said she could handle it and shooed me off to lunch. Sit down. Or do you think it would look too much like collusion with the enemy?"

"So who's an enemy? Besides, I can collude with whoever I please. Whomever," I corrected. "Just in case Ms. Evans is listening."

Jordan groaned. "She's a bear on grammar, isn't she?"

I couldn't believe I was having a conversation with Jordan, just as if we were the best of friends who shared the miseries of an English class.

Setting my tray on the table, I sat down. Now that my lunch was right there in front of Jordan's nose, it seemed very embarrassing. I had a hot dog without a bun, and the naked wienie lay there on my plate, slathered with a gob of mustard. I had a scoop of limp salad, and I noticed that some of the lettuce leaves had brown edges. French fries lay in a greasy heap on one side of my plate. The only other things I had were a carton of milk and a straw to drink it with.

My food all seemed so personal. And so hazardous. I would probably dribble mustard down my front. I would end up with a piece of brown-edged lettuce leaf stuck to a front tooth. I would slurp my milk as I sucked it through the straw. Why was it *everything* embarrassed me when Jordan was around?

Jordan didn't seem to be embarrassed by his food. Picking up a piece of pizza, dripping with melted cheese, he gnawed off a big hunk. After working it around in his mouth, he swallowed and then asked, "How's it going, Trish? Do you have your speech ready for the assembly tomorrow?"

"Needs a little polishing." Carefully I cut into the wienie so it wouldn't shoot off my plate.

"You'll do fine," Jordan said around another bite of pizza. "Speech-making is your thing."

So he *had* noticed me before I entered the election. But he hadn't asked me for a date—at some future time—until I had proved myself as a candidate. I was doing everything right!

"Thanks," I said, "but I'll have to go some to be as good as you."

"Oh, I don't know. The main thing I'm going to do is have this ghost swoop down from the rafters on some wires, and I'll introduce him as our school spirit. Then I'll kind of wing it from there."

Why was he telling me what he was going to do? To intimidate me, as R. G. said? But what did it hurt if I knew?

"You've really surprised me, Trish," Jordan was saying, wiping pizza crumbs from his lips with a paper napkin, which he dropped beside his plate. I wanted to snatch it up and take it home with me where I would preserve it in a box somewhere. Then years later, when he was governor and I was the first lady of the state, known far and wide for my beautiful quilts, I would show him that crumpled napkin and tell him how I had felt during that first meal we had shared. And he would smile and say, "Yes, I remember. That's when I first told you how much I admired your quilts."

Only it wasn't quilts he was talking about.

"I really admire your super imagination," he was saying. "You know, when you first entered the election, I thought it would be a sure thing to beat you. Now I know it's going to be harder than I thought."

I noticed he didn't say it might not happen. Just that it would be harder than he thought.

"I always knew you'd be a tough opponent," I said honestly.

He smiled. "Trish, whatever happens, we'll still be friends, won't we? In fact, I'd like to get together as soon as we can and make plans for next year."

"Next year?"

He nodded, swallowing another bite of pizza. "I'm going to run for Associated Student Body president next year, and I'd like to have you run as vice-president. We'd be a dynamite team, Trish. In more ways than one."

I should have just smiled sweetly and said I'd think about it. But maybe it was that line of gallant female ancestors prodding me that made me say, "What if I should win, Jordan? What if I should run for Associated Student Body president next year? Would you run as vice-president?"

Jordan didn't answer right away. He pushed his plate aside. He shredded his napkin, that keepsake napkin I had planned to preserve.

"Trish," he said finally, "I have ambitions."

"I have ambitions, too, Jordan."

Hadn't I already heard this scenario? For a minute it

154

seemed like one of those déjà vu things where you think you have lived through a particular moment before. But then I realized it was almost a replay of the scene between Dannalee's parents on Monday.

Jordan sat silent for a while again, and then reached over and put his hand over mine. "Trish, don't be mad, but I have to tell you this. I couldn't run as vice-president. I couldn't take second place."

I wasn't mad. Some women like macho men who insist on being the boss.

The thing was, I wasn't sure I was one of those women.

On the other hand, I couldn't be sure I wasn't, either.

I was so mixed-up. I sat there wishing he would take me into his arms, smooth my hair, tell me again what a dynamite team we could be.

Fickle, fickle me. The night before, I had wanted R. G. to take me into *his* arms.

One thing I knew. If love was like an election, then I wasn't ready to vote.

Jordan stood up. "Thanks for having lunch with me, Trish. I'll be in touch after the voting."

For the second time in three days, I watched a guy walk away from me. Picking up the shredded napkin Jordan had left behind, I thought about how everything I had done in my campaign had been connected to my love for him.

Getting up, I walked to the trash can and dropped the napkin into it along with my half-eaten, cold frankfurter, the empty milk carton, and other things I didn't want anymore.

16

WHEN WE GOT TO SCHOOL the next morning, we found that
somebody had been busy with our bash signs. They had been
altered so that instead of announcing "Bash Belch in the
parking lot at noon," they said "Trash Trish in the parking lot at noon." It was easy to figure out who did it.

"Forget it," I said when R. G. started to haul down one
of the signs. "Maybe that will bring a bigger crowd than
bashing Belch."

R. G. grinned. "Could be. By the way, you're going to
take the first swing at Belch, you know."

"Oh, no, not me," I protested. "I'm not going anywhere
near that little party."

"Sure, you are," R. G. insisted. "You have to be there.
Sort of symbolic, you know, striking the first blow for the
junior-class treasury."

"Think of Belch." Dannalee cast her eyes piously heav-
enward. "Belch would have wanted it that way."

"Oh, Dannalee, don't be gross." I sighed. "Okay, I'll do it."

The three of us—along with Snyde—had driven to Pratt squeezed into the cab of R. G.'s dad's pickup truck. Now R. G. took hold of Snyde's collar and towed him off toward the woodworking shop, where he would spend the morning.

"See you at noon," R. G. said.

By the time Dannalee and I got to the parking lot after our eleven o'clock class, R. G. had everything ready to go. Snyde was there with his blond curls tied firmly to his head. R. G. had draped Dannalee's shawl around him again, and he was a very convincing Aunt Beulah. He was sitting on the hood of Belch, enjoying the attention of the kids who came up to pet him. R. G. stood by the car tooting his tuba. Every time R. G. hit a note higher than usual, Snyde howled. Altogether, it was a good act.

There were lots more people there than I had expected. It looked as if most of the student body had come to bash Belch. Or trash Trish.

Jordan wasn't there, and I was glad of that. Susu was. She stood there casually sipping from a tall red Coca-Cola cup. She was like a big spider surrounded by all the little flies she had caught in her web. When she saw me coming, she started them all chanting, "Trash Trish. Trash Trish."

R. G. had had my treasure chest locked up somewhere since the opening day of the campaign, but now it was sitting there on a rickety little table with the sign saying, "The best is in the chest."

I was still worried about that chest.

"Do you think the kids are going to be mad when I show

them my treasure chest is empty after all the hype?" I asked Dannalee.

"Not so loud, " Dannalee whispered. "Susu is headed this way."

I turned to see Susu and her flies almost upon us.

"Hi, Trish," Susu said. She eyed my treasure chest. "What do you *really* have in there, dog biscuits?"

"Yeah, would you like one?" Dannalee asked.

Susu smiled sweetly. "Well, I can tell you this much. There's *nothing* in that stupid chest that can beat Jordan."

Dannalee smiled just as sweetly. "Then what are you so worried about, Susu?"

Susu's smile puckered as if she'd just sucked a lemon. "If you think I'm worried about Trish *or* her stupid treasure chest, you're crazy." As she turned to leave, her hip bumped against the rickety little table that held my treasure chest. I can't say she meant to do it, but I can't say she didn't mean to, either. At any rate, the table fell over and the chest crashed to the pavement. The rusty old hinges broke, and the lid came partway off. Stacks of what looked like foot-long dollar bills spilled out.

"Hey, look," somebody yelled, and kids started grabbing for the big bucks, pushing Susu and the flies aside.

I snatched one myself. It was like an enormous dollar bill, only instead of George Washington's picture, *my* picture was printed on it.

So that was why R. G. had wanted a photo of me.

I faced Dannalee, waving the big buck. "Do you know anything about this? What's going on, anyway?"

She looked pleased with herself. "R. G. and I figured we'd put the 'best in the chest,' just like the sign says. Look what it says on the bill."

I looked at the big buck I held in my hand. " 'The real treasure of Pratt High is Trish,' " I read. "Oh, Dannalee, this is embarrassing. If I had known you were doing this, I wouldn't have let you."

Dannalee shrugged. "Exactly why we didn't tell you. It's true, Trish. Why not say it?" She looked at the kids scrambling for the bills. "There's enough for everyone," she yelled. "Pass them around." Turning back to me, she said, "We almost didn't get these ready in time. The *Pratt Blatt* ran them off for us yesterday."

A light dawned. "Is that why you and R. G. sneaked off uptown?" The light grew brighter. "Is that why you've had your heads together so much lately?"

"Sure," Dannalee said. "Did you think we were having a big love affair or something?"

My tattletale face flamed.

Dannalee looked shocked. "Are you crazy, Trish? How do you think I could make time with R. G. when all he can see is you?" She grinned at me. "Not that I didn't try!"

"Hey, wait a minute," I said. I wanted to think about this a minute, to think about R. G., who couldn't see anybody else but me. It didn't make sense. But of course it did. That's why he had been working so hard to get me to realize my own potential.

Suddenly I was ashamed of myself. I had suspected R. G. of having all kinds of devious motives. Was it possible that his only motive was that he loved me?

Somebody was rattling one of the big bucks in my face. "Hey," he said, "can I buy three bashes with one of these bucks?"

It brought my mind back to the car bash. "Better go

check with Gordie Coons," I told him. "He's taking the money."

I looked around for R. G. He was standing by Belch, rubbing a fender gently. "We'd better get on with this," I told Dannalee.

"Yeah, it's almost time for the assembly." She started gathering up the broken treasure chest. "I'm sorry Susu ruined this before your big speech. I wanted to see your face when you went to show an empty chest and all those big bucks fell out."

I didn't mind missing that. "I'll say my secret campaign promise is just that I'll do my very best to be a good president if I'm elected." I was watching R. G. standing there saying good-bye to his car.

As I watched, he gave it a final pat, and then put down his tuba and lifted Snyde from Belch's hood. He picked up the sledgehammer he had brought with us that morning.

Holding up a hand for silence, he said, "We're here today to get a good start on building the biggest junior-class treasury in the history of Pratt High. Trish is going to start it off."

I wished I could stop this whole thing. But Gordie Coons had a whole stack of dollar bills from people who had bought three bashes for a buck. I had to do it.

Up to that point, I hadn't looked much at Belch. But now I had to. R. G. had rolled all the windows down and taken out the headlights so there wouldn't be any flying glass. He was going to break the windshield out himself after I struck the first blow.

Belch crouched there, waiting like a beautiful virgin maiden ready to be sacrificed. Its blue paint was polished. Its chrome gleamed.

R. G. handed the sledgehammer to me.

I took it, thinking how much R. G. had invested in his car. Time, money, effort. Love.

- I hefted the hammer. The blind headlight sockets stared at me.

"I can't do it," I whispered to R. G.

"Do it," he whispered back. His eyes were shut.

Susu and her crew were standing nearby. "Trash Trish," one of them said.

Come on, I told myself. *Remember what Marv said. If you're going to compete with the barracudas, you have to do the things the barracudas do.*

No, I argued with myself. *If I have to do that, the price is too high.*

Flinging the hammer aside, I looked at all the waiting faces. "I'm sorry," I said. "This car is a personal friend. Bashing it would be kind of like an act of violence. I don't want to build our class treasury that way."

"I'll do it if she's too chicken," Susu yelled. "I'll get Jordan to do it."

"No," I said, standing close to Belch. "Nobody is going to do it."

R. G. was looking down at me. "This might cost you a lot of votes, Trish."

I listened to the muttering around us. "Maybe. Look, R. G., you can take Belch home and keep it around until you can afford to fix it up. You said yourself it could be a classic someday. You don't want to ruin it now."

"I would for you, Trish."

I didn't have time to answer because just then Snyde shot out of the parking lot. He still wore his wig, and Dannalee's shawl flapped behind him as he ran.

"Snyde!" I yelled. I looked around at the assembled crowd. "What happened to him?"

"I don't know," Dannalee said. "He was visiting around with everybody, and then all of a sudden he started shaking his head and took off."

"We'd better go after him," R. G. said. Fitting action to words, he sprinted off.

"Oh, Snyde," I said, getting my own feet in gear. He was just a big old farm dog. He didn't know the hazards of a town.

Hazards—Traxler!

"Snyde," I wailed.

By the thunder of feet behind me, I knew that most of the student body of Pratt High was joining in the chase. I guess they didn't want to miss anything.

When I got to the street, I couldn't see Snyde. But a couple of people passing by were staring in the direction of Main Street, so I knew Snyde had gone that way. R. G. was headed that way, too.

Just before I got to Main Street, I heard a screech of brakes, and my heart dropped. But when I rounded the corner, I saw Snyde streaking off ahead, with R. G. close behind him. A car was stalled kind of crosswise on the street. The driver looked pale.

"I almost hit a little old lady," he said. "She was running on all fours."

Ahead of us, Snyde was squatting down, scratching vigorously at his wig with a back foot. Just before R. G. got to him, he shot off again.

That's when Traxler came ambling out of the Pratt Cafe, picking his teeth after a big lunch. The first thing he spotted was Snyde rocketing toward him, his curls bouncing and his shawl flapping.

Traxler tensed, crouching down like the gunfighters in the oat operas on TV. His hand dropped to that big ugly pistol he always wears slung around his hips.

"No!" R. G. hollered.

Traxler looked up to see most of the student body of Pratt High bearing down on him. Evidently he had second thoughts about hauling out that pistol because his hand fell away from it and he stood up, assuming a karate stance. He stared at Snyde.

"What the hell *is* it?" he bellowed.

"A dog," R. G. yelled back. "It's just a dog."

By now Snyde had slowed to a walk. His tongue hung out, dripping spit as he panted.

"Everybody stand back," Traxler commanded. "He's got rabies or something." He changed positions, getting a big booted foot ready to kick Snyde if he attacked.

"He won't hurt you," R. G. called. He was getting close to Snyde now, with the rest of us right behind him.

"He sure as hell won't." Traxler was prepared for anything. His face was red, and he looked as if he were sweating. He kept his eyes glued on the dog as Synde walked up to him, sat down, and offered a paw to shake hands.

"Nice doggie," Traxler said weakly, wilting against the window of the Pratt Cafe.

R. G. arrived and stood by Snyde, putting a protective hand on his head.

Traxler's bristle came back. "Oh, it's you," he said to R. G. He flicked a finger at Snyde. "This the same mutt I told you snots to keep out of town?"

Gordie Coons pounded up and skidded to a stop. "I know what happened." He gasped for breath. "Susu did it. She put ice cubes under Snyde's wig. That's why he went crazy."

Quickly I untied the wig and took it off Snyde. His big head was wet and dripping, but the evidence had melted.

Traxler sighed. "The three of you." He pointed to R. G., Snyde, and me. "Come along. I'm taking you in this time."

We were hauled off in the cop car in front of most of the student body of Pratt High and a lot of the townspeople, who had gathered to watch.

Traxler took us to the courthouse, but he didn't keep us very long. Since I was going to be a lawyer someday, this was a good chance to practice. My speech to Traxler was a masterpiece, if I do say so myself. I pleaded Snyde's case, I explained my part in it, I declared R. G.'s innocence. I ended up complimenting Traxler on the cool way he handled the whole situation. Then I presented him with the big buck with my picture on it that I still clutched in my hand.

Traxler was impressed with my speech. "You got a real mouth on you," he said.

Damn the barracudas, full speed ahead. I could handle them in my own way.

Traxler drove us back to the high school. All the way there, he lectured us on keeping our noses clean in the future.

In the backseat, where Snyde was panting his poisonous breath all around us, I said, "I'm going to win, R. G."

He looked at me. "You've always had my vote, Trish." And right there in Traxler's cop car, he pulled me to his rock-hard chest, bent his head, and kissed me. This time it was right out of one of Dannalee's mother's romances.

I was wrong. Snyde won the election. Almost ninety percent of next year's junior class wrote in Aunt Beulah as their choice for president. He doesn't want to serve, though, so we're going to have a runoff election.

But isn't that the way life is—just one choice after another?